ALL THE
WORLD'S
A STAGE

ALL THE WORLD'S A STAGE

A Novel in Five Acts

by Gretchen Woelfle

illustrated by
Thomas Cox

Holiday House / New York

JF
WOE

Library of Congress Cataloging-in-Publication Data

Woelfle, Gretchen.

All the world's a stage : a novel in five acts / by Gretchen Woelfle. — 1st ed.

p. cm.

Summary: Twelve-year-old orphan Christopher "Kit" Buckles becomes a stage boy in a London theater in 1598, tries his hand at acting, and later helps build the Globe Theater for playwright William Shakespeare and the Chamberlain's Men acting troupe.

ISBN 978-0-8234-2281-4 (hardcover)

[1. Theater—Fiction. 2. Apprentices—Fiction. 3. Actors and actresses— Fiction. 4. Shakespeare, William, 1564-1616—Fiction. 5. Chamberlain's Men (Theater company)—Fiction. 6. Globe Theatre (London, England : 1599-1644)— Fiction. 7. Great Britain—History—Elizabeth, 1558-1603—Fiction.] I. Title.

PZ7.W8173All 2011

[Fic]—dc22

201 0023474

To Alice

CONTENTS

ACKNOWLEDGMENTS

This book has been a most joyful adventure, with many goodly encounters along the way. Marvin Close, July Oskar Cole, Jesse Graham, Carolyn Marsden, and Cleo Woelfle-Erskine read early drafts and kept me on the path. Tobin Anderson served as a wondrous guide to Elizabethan music. James Shapiro's book A *Year in the Life of William Shakespeare: 1599* provided an almost daily account of the activities of the Lord Chamberlain's Men. In addition, Professor Shapiro swiftly responded to my e-mails, supplying even more information about when and how things happened. I thank Louise Curren for the backstage tour of Shakespeare's Globe Theatre, and Julie Tancell at the Worshipful Company of Carpenters for sharing some colorful history. David, Emily, and others were brilliant guides on several walking tours of Shakespeare's London. A heartfelt thanks to Eleni Beja for taking on Kit & Co. and to Julie Amper for her editing prowess. Thomas Cox's illustrations are a dream come true. Finally I want to thank my daughter, Alice Woelfle-Erskine, for hosting me on several trips to London, lending me one of her bicycles, and accompanying me hither and yon — remember the Elizabethan Hunting Lodge in Epping Forest? — as I delved into Kit's world.

These Be the Names of the Players

Kit Buckles — runaway orphan

Molly Godden — apple-seller at the playhouse

Roger — leader of a gang of cutpurses

Tom — stage-keeper

Giles Allen — owner of the land beneath the Theatre

Henry Johnson — friend of Giles Allen

Lord Chamberlain's Men

William Shakespeare — playwright

Richard Burbage — leading player

Cuthbert Burbage — business manager

Will Kemp — clown/fool

Augustine Phillips — player, musician

James Sands — apprentice player

Nicholas Tooley — apprentice player

CARPENTERS

Peter Street — master carpenter; member of Worshipful Company

of Carpenters guild

Samuel — carpenter, not yet a master

ACT FIRST, SCENE I

Cutpurse

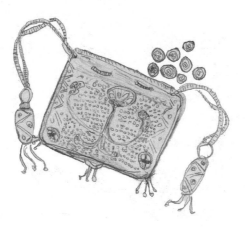

"Boy! Pay your penny!" The money-gatherer grabbed for Kit, but he ducked between two men and darted through the crowd to the middle of the Theatre. When he looked back, he saw the gatherer busy taking money once more.

Fear and excitement roiled in Kit's belly.

"Fires and sprites!" he exclaimed as he looked around. Three stories tall the Theatre stood, taller than a church, shaped like a huge egg, and open to the sky. Ladies and gentlemen made their way upstairs to the seats in the galleries around the edge. Common folk — groundlings — stood on the dirt floor, pushing past Kit to get near the stage. Marble columns held up the stage roof that was painted with stars to look like the night sky.

Brrm, ba ba brrm! A trumpet sounded.

A man dressed in fine clothes walked to the front of the stage and began to speak about the king and his troubles. The play had begun, the first Kit had ever seen. The audience grew quiet as more players appeared, strutting and stumbling, shouting and muttering. Kit leaned forward to hear every word. Suddenly two men onstage drew their swords and began slashing at each other.

"Villain!" the groundlings shouted.

"Watch right!"

"Scurvy cur!"

"Kill 'im!"

Kit gasped. The two swordsmen looked for all the world like they meant to murder each other.

"You be not here to watch the play, you witless ninnyhammer," hissed a voice in Kit's ear.

He spun around to see Roger looming over him. "I ... I am waiting for a good moment."

"Liar," said Roger. "I see you gawping at the play. Get you to work! Fight scenes be the best time to nip a bung!"

Roger spoke truly. Kit had got caught up in the play. He took one more look at the stage and saw that a swordsman was down. Blood spread across his shirt, but he still had breath for a dying speech.

"I said, get you to work!" Roger yanked Kit's yellow curls.

"Ow!" squawked Kit, rubbing his head.

Shrinking away from Roger, Kit moved through the crowd.

His stomach churned as he looked for small purses — bungs — tied to men's belts. The crowd was so packed he could see only heads and shoulders. Kit drew his knife from his boot. His hands shook.

Quick as a flea jumps off a dog, Kit cut the cord holding a man's purse, caught it as it fell, slipped it up his sleeve, and crept away. Just as Roger had taught him. He grinned at Roger, but Roger wasn't watching.

"Apples, apples, who will buy of me!" a girl sang out. Kit's mouth felt dry, but he had no money of his own. He had to give the purse to Roger.

A troop of dancers burst onto the stage. A lute played to the beat of a drum, and men and women danced about. People in the audience began to clap in time with the music. Kit spotted more purses now. He took out his knife and cut another one. It clinked as he tucked it into his sleeve.

Should he leave, or try for one more? A playhouse was easier than the street market, where you never knew when a man would reach for his money. One more, and then he would go. Or maybe he would stay to watch the end of the play. He quite fancied seeing another sword fight.

A couple walked past, and he saw a fat purse at the man's side. Swift as you please, Kit slit the cord and felt the purse drop into his hands. He slid it up his sleeve as he bent down to hide his knife in his boot.

Suddenly a hand gripped the back of his neck. "Cutpurse!" the money-gatherer shouted.

Kit tried to break free as people turned to look.

"Cutpurse!" the man cried again.

Men clutched their sides.

"He did not get mine."

"Mine be gone...."

"The rapscallion...."

"Insolent brat...."

"Take that, you rotten thief!"

"Ouch!" Kit cried as nutshells stung his head.

The money-gatherer grabbed Kit around the middle, lifted him off the ground, and shook him. Kit's arms went slack, and three purses fell to the floor. He flailed and kicked. The heel of his boot hit the gatherer's shin.

"Owww!" the man cried as he dropped Kit, who slipped past others trying to grab him.

Thud! His head hit the ground, and he saw stars. He tried to stand.

Umph. He fell again, got a mouthful of ashes, and spit them out. Once more he tried to get up, but he was pinned to the ground. When he lifted his head, he saw the apple girl sitting on his back. Kit struggled to get free, but she did not budge.

"Over here!" she called. "I caught the cutpurse!"

Kit saw Roger slink out the door without looking his way. Who would help him now?

Prisoner

Kit tugged at the rope that bound his hands. The gatherer had taken him to the room behind the stage and given him over to a burly man named Tom, who tied Kit's hands around a post.

Tom said, "Be glad you be not tied to a pillar on the stage. They would throw rotten fruit at you then. If you make the smallest noise, I'll bind your mouth too."

Kit kept still. He heard swords clashing, girls chattering, and men shouting. Back in this room, three doorways led to the stage, and costumes were spread on tables. Players rushed in, changed costumes, and ran out again. One boy asked, "Who is he?"

"The cutpurse what did spoil Mr. Richard's big speech in Act I," Tom answered.

The boy scowled at Kit. "Mr. Richard will have your head on a spike on London Bridge. Stealing purses be bad enough, but spoiling his speech is much worse."

"I did not mean to...." Kit began, but the boy had gone. Was it true? Would he lose his head for cutting three purses? His heart thumped so hard it made his ears ring. He barely heard the final applause from the audience.

All the players burst into the room, dressed like servant girls and fine ladies, grand soldiers and rough countrymen. They chattered about who had missed his lines and how one lad had tripped over his skirt and nearly bumped into the king. Kit was surprised to see that boys had played the women's parts.

Then the king himself swept in, and everyone moved aside to let him pass. "Be this the scoundrel who interrupted my speech?" he roared, glaring at Kit.

"'Tis he, Mr. Richard," said the boy who had frightened Kit earlier. "You should have seen —"

"Silence, Nicholas!"

Kit looked up at the stout man. He was not a king, only a player. England had a queen, not a king, but Queen Elizabeth herself could not be more frightening.

"Sir, I —" Kit began, but his tongue froze, and his chest heaved as he tried to breathe.

"Unbind the boy before he faints," said Mr. Richard.

"Faints like a girl," sneered Nicholas as he untied the rope. "'Twas a girl who caught him. Molly tripped him and then sat on him."

Everyone laughed as Kit sank onto a bench. He pinched his lips together. These were not kings and soldiers, just players pretending to be brave heroes. He would show them who was brave. He threw himself into a forest of legs and dashed toward the door.

Thump! He fell down hard.

"You again!" cried the apple girl, who sat on his stomach this time.

Kit groaned. Tom and another man grabbed his arms. Kit twisted and turned, but the men dragged him back to the middle of the room. When Molly came near, he saw she was no taller than he. He glared at her.

"You will stay here and attend to Mr. Richard," growled Tom.

Richard Burbage, whose voice could reach every seat in the playhouse and halfway to heaven, boomed, "Or would you rather we give you to the sheriff?"

Kit shook his head. "No, sir."

"What is your name?"

"Kit."

Mr. Richard glowered.

"Christopher Buckles, sir."

"You were caught cutting purses at the play today?"

Kit cringed. "Yes, sir."

"How old are you? Where do you live?"

"I am new to London, sir. Twelve, I be twelve."

"You be rather small for twelve and ill-fed. Where was your home?"

"Suffolk, sir, Aldeburgh." Kit stood still as a statue and bowed his head.

A shorter man with a beard came forward. "He speaks truly, Richard. I know it from his speech." He walked up to Kit. "We did play in Aldeburgh a few summers ago. 'Tis a lovely village on the sea. Your family lives there?"

Kit raised his eyes just enough to see the man's face through his own tousled hair. "My mother died giving birth to me, sir. Dad was a fisherman, until he was lost in a storm...." Kit was shamed to feel tears filling his eyes.

"Go on," said the man. He had a kind voice.

"I lived with my grandame and grandsire then."

Richard Burbage turned to the bearded man and said, "There you go again, learning the story of everyone you meet. This urchin will show up in your next play, I trow." He laughed and took off his crown.

"Perchance he will," the other man replied. Then he turned to Kit. "Was your grandsire a fisherman, too?"

Kit sat tall. "No, sir, he was a master shipwright. He built ships for the Queen's Navy that beat the Spanish Armada." Kit stuck out his chin. "He said if 'twere not for the shipwrights of Suffolk we would all speak Spanish now."

The bearded man chuckled. "Did he? I could not make my living writing plays in Spanish, so I thank your grandsire. Will you tell him that for me?"

Kit frowned. Was this man making fun of him? He lowered his eyes. "Grannie and Grandsire died of the fever last winter."

"And you ran away to London to make your fortune, like a hundred thousand other boys."

Kit stared at the man.

"How did you live then, Kit?"

"I was on my own, until I met Roger —" Kit broke off. 'Twas a mistake to name Roger. He might be a clumsy cutpurse, but he was not a snitch.

Richard Burbage broke in. "And he taught you to be a cutpurse?"

Kit shook his head. "I taught me myself."

"That part of your education is finished, if you know what is good for you. The question now is — How should you be punished?"

Kit's eyes widened.

Mr. Richard went on. "I am told that your three victims got their money back, but you did commit a crime. We should give you over to the sheriff."

"Will he cut off my head and put it on a spike on London Bridge, sir?" Kit's voice broke.

Nicholas laughed, but Mr. Richard said, "Silence. No, he will not do that — unless you plan a revolt against the Queen." He raised an eyebrow.

Kit stammered, "Oh no, sir. I do not, sir."

"The sheriff might beat you or put you in a dungeon with the rats. Or perhaps he will send you off to that savage wilderness they call Virginia. Which would you prefer?"

"None of it, sir," Kit whispered. He could hardly speak.

The man with the beard asked, "How much money was in the purses he cut?"

Molly, the apple girl, piped up. "Twelve shillings and eightpence. I saw the men count it, to be sure none was missing."

"A stage boy would work more than a month to earn that sum in bed and board."

Nicholas added, "And get fined for interrupting Mr. Richard's speech."

"'Tis so, Nicholas," replied the bearded man. "It appears you owe us six weeks of work, Kit. Either that or pay a visit to the sheriff." He turned to Tom. "Can you use a stage boy?"

"If he will work," said Tom, frowning at Kit.

"Richard?"

He shrugged. "Backstage is not my concern."

The bearded man's gaze swept the room until he found a tall handsome man. "Augustine, do you have room in your house for one more boy?"

"He can share him a bed with James."

The bearded man looked at Kit sternly. "We offer you bed and board with Augustine Phillips, in exchange for six weeks' work with Tom, our stage-keeper — and your word of honor to our company of players, the Lord Chamberlain's Men."

Kit reddened under that look. They were tossing him about like a cat tosses a mouse. He stared at the ground. He did not want to be given over to the sheriff, but he did not want to be a prisoner here either. They could not keep him tied up all the time. If they did, he could not work. As soon as he could, he would run away, back to Roger.

"Do not think of going back to Roger," the man with the beard said.

Kit stared. Could this man hear his thoughts?

"You are no use to him now that your face be known to us and all the groundlings who pelted you with nutshells."

The players laughed, but the man did not. "If you do go back, you may end up face down in the River Thames like many a failed criminal. That is not the fate your grandsire wanted for you when he built those ships."

Kit slumped onto a bench. How dare this man read his mind and tell him what to do, then make him ashamed of what he had done! How could he do all that with a few words?

The man went on. "The town of Aldeburgh gave us a banquet after our play, in the town hall near the sea. I remember the summer sky heaped with clouds over the water, all of them soft glowing shades of blue. I have never seen the like of it, before or since. Do you remember those skies, Kit?"

Kit did not answer.

He went on. "I came to London, just like you, because I wanted more than my native town could give me. But we should not forget from where and whom we come. Your people were hardworking and honest."

Kit, soothed by the kind voice, raised his eyes.

"Here is a chance to prove that you are, too."

Kit thought of the hungry days he had suffered when he first came to London. 'Twas nearly November now, and the nights were growing long and cold. He might stay at the playhouse — as long as that Nicholas cove and that Molly wench did not torment him.

Finally he spoke. "I will work for the Lord Chamberlain's Men."

Richard Burbage took off his kingly cloak. "Will Shakespeare doth weave a wily web of words once more."

Will Shakespeare held out his hand to Kit, who shook it. "Kit Buckles, you have spirit. Shipwrights, playwrights, country boys new to London — no one gets far without that."

Kit wondered, had his spirit got him into this plight? Would it get him out again?

Drudge

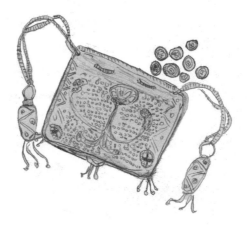

"Be quick, boy," barked Tom. "When you be finished sweeping the stage, help Nicholas and James sort out the costumes. Then clean the ground. 'Tis a right swamp after the rain last night."

Kit scowled. He had been working at the playhouse for a week, but it seemed like a month. 'Twas sometimes dull, as now, sweeping the stage; sometimes irksome, cleaning petticoats and breeches; and sometimes most filthy, picking up rotten fruit and other rubbish the audience tossed away. Worst of all was hauling great sacks of ashes and sand, mixing them with hazelnut shells, and spreading the whole mess on the muddy ground where people would just throw their rubbish.

"Step aside, lad, we are here to rehearse." Richard Burbage swept onto the stage with Will Shakespeare. Kit leaned on his broom. If he left now, Tom would berate him for not finishing the work.

"Should I do the sweeping later, sir?" Kit asked.

"Am I a stage-keeper?" Mr. Richard bellowed.

"He is just trying to do his job, Richard," said Will Shakespeare.

"And I, to do mine."

Will Shakespeare said, "Finish sweeping later, Kit. We are rehearsing a new play and that makes us all testy." He glanced at Mr. Richard.

"Yes, sir," said Kit, hiding a smile.

"Can we get on with the scene?" demanded Mr. Richard as Kit walked away.

Kit stopped and listened to the two men. He could not grasp much of the story, but he was taken by the rhythm of the words and Mr. Richard's strong clear voice. Will Shakespeare read lines too, but his voice was not so strong. Kit had not seen him since that first day, yet he had remembered Kit's name.

"You lazy cove!"

Kit jumped at the sound of Tom's voice.

"Mr. Richard wanted to rehearse —"

"No excuses. Go you and help the other boys!" Tom glared at Kit, who headed back to the tiring house.

The first day Tom had ordered him to find Nicholas in the tiring house, Kit had left the playhouse to look for a house where Nicholas had retired to rest. Nicholas had found him wandering about and nearly split his breeches laughing when he heard Kit's explanation.

"'Tis a good jest," Nicholas sputtered. "The *retiring* house —

would we not like one of those! No, you clod, the tiring house is the room behind the stage where we set out the costumes, the attire. 'Tis the *attire* house, the tiring house." Nicholas laughed again.

How would Kit know that? He thumped his broom on the ground, remembering how angry he had felt. Three meals a day and a dry bed in the attic. Were they reward enough for being the butt of people's jokes and obeying their wretched commands all day long? He was everyone's drudge.

On the streets he had had freedom. Freedom to wander wherever he liked. To work for a few hours for a wherryman or a fruit-seller in exchange for a meat pie or a penny to buy one, then to watch the jugglers on Fleet Street or the boats that went up and down the River Thames, until he wanted another meal. Then he had met Roger and lived with his gang. 'Tis true, cutting purses was a frightening and shameful trade, but Roger and his boys had been good fun. Not like Nicholas who bullied him or ignored him altogether.

Nicholas and James looked up when Kit entered the room. They were arranging boots, dresses, and wigs for the afternoon play.

"Tom told me to help you," Kit muttered.

"You could wash the blood off this shirt," said James, holding it up.

"Is it real blood?" asked Kit, examining the brown stain down the front.

"'Tis the blood of a pig," said James, "hidden in a bladder inside the shirt. The player squeezes it when he is struck by a rapier."

"We do not need his help," broke in Nicholas as he combed the curls of a lady's wig.

"We do if we want our dinner today," said James. "There is your dress to sew, three bloody shirts to wash, and four weapons to polish —"

"I will polish the swords," said Kit. He had wanted to see those since the first day.

"They are rapiers, not swords, and you will not polish them," snapped Nicholas. "You will wash the bloody shirts."

"You are not my master. You do not tell me what to do!"

"So the cutpurse puts on airs, does he?" Nicholas set the wig on his head and flung his arms out like a grand lady, as he did on the stage.

"Stow you, Nicholas," said James.

"The cutpurse thinks he can order milady about!" Nicholas danced toward Kit and chucked him under the chin. "We are apprentice players, James and I. You are just a stage boy, and a daft one at that."

Kit grabbed Nicholas's arm and twisted it. James flicked a towel at them. Kit felt a sting and let go. James, who was just ten but nearly as tall as Kit, jumped between the older boys. "Do you want to be charged with extra work? I do not. Hold your tongue, Nicholas, and keep your temper, Kit."

Nicholas twirled around in his wig once more without speaking. Then he sat down and began to let out the hem of his dress for the afternoon's play.

James showed Kit how to scrub the bloodstain with ammonia and water.

"Phew, it stinks!" said Kit.

James laughed. "It does the job though. Just stop breathing for a while."

Nicholas snickered and Kit frowned as he scrubbed the shirt.

A few minutes later, Will Shakespeare came into the room. "Nicholas, we need you for the court scene."

"Yes, sir," said Nicholas, but his voice cracked on the last word. He pulled off the lady's wig and flung it in Kit's face. Kit sat stunned. Then he dove for Nicholas, catching him round the knees and crashing into the table. Dresses and doublets tumbled to the floor, and the two boys fell on top of them. Kit pinned Nicholas's arms as Nicholas wrestled to get free.

"Nicholas! Kit!" Will Shakespeare shouted. "Stop! At once!"

"Where is that wretched boy?" Richard Burbage burst through the door and stared at the tangle of boys and costumes. "How dare you!" he thundered.

Kit released Nicholas, and both boys stood up. "Two weeks' cleaning the ground for you, Nicholas, more — much more — if those costumes are damaged!" Richard Burbage peered at Kit. "Are you not the cutpurse? I do not know why we did not give you to the sheriff. Two weeks more you will work for us."

"Richard, we must rehearse," said Will Shakespeare, frowning at Kit as he led Richard and Nicholas out of the room.

James began to pick up the costumes from the floor. "That was the worst thing you could have done."

"Worse than ruining a speech?" muttered Kit, snatching the wig Nicholas had flung at him.

"Hmm, they are both grievous bad." James brushed off a lady's gown. "Most of the company's profits go to pay for costumes."

Kit glowered. "I do not care. Nicholas deserved it."

"Nicholas is not easy, even in good times, and now 'tis a most bad time for him," James said.

"A bad time? He plays the best ladies' roles, and people clap for him every day." Kit flung a pair of boots on top of a pile of doublets. James picked them up and set them on the floor. Kit gave them a kick.

James said, "He is grown so much he barely fits any of the dresses. I see him plucking hairs from his chin every morning. But worst of all, his voice is changing. He is nearly seventeen, and he cannot play a lady much longer."

"That does not give him the right to treat me as he does."

James sighed. "I am not taking his side. I am just trying to explain."

"What will happen to him? Will he be out on the street?"

"He is a marvelous good player, so when he cannot play a lady, he will play men's parts. But he will not get the leading roles as long as Mr. Richard is here. Nicholas likes the applause he gets now."

Kit looked at James. He was years away from a beard. "'Tis good for you, then. You will play his parts."

"'Tis not what I want though...." James began.

Tom poked his head in the door. "Everything be ready for this afternoon?"

"Yes, sir," said James.

"Good lad," said Tom, smiling. His smile vanished when he saw Kit. "Did you not clean the ground yet? 'Tis dinnertime, but you will not get yours until you do." He hurried away.

"Do not mind Tom," said James. "He blows hot and cold in a moment."

But Kit did mind. Nicholas and James were signed apprentices, learning a trade. He was just a cutpurse, a daft drudge, to be ordered about. And now he had two weeks added to his sentence.

He picked up a sack to collect the rubbish and walked out to the stage. The players had gone to the inn for dinner. Kit stood in the center of the stage. The columns that he thought at first were marble were just painted wood, not as grand up close as they looked from the audience, not grand at all. The paint was chipped and peeling.

Kit looked at the seats rising up, up, up. 'Twas where the ladies and gentlemen sat, clapping for Mr. Richard and Nicholas, even for James. They would never applaud him. Not that he cared. He did not belong in this hive of arrogant kings and prating bullies. He would not be their prisoner, not for another minute. He would rather take his chances on the street. Kit jumped off the stage, dropped the sack in the mud, and ran for the door.

ACT SECOND

Runaway

Kit did not stop running until he was half a mile down Shoreditch Road, nearly to Bishopsgate, where the wall of the city of London rose up. Inside that wall, he was safe. The crowds of people, narrow winding lanes, and jumble of market stalls would hide him from anyone from the playhouse who might come looking. But what did they care about a runaway cutpurse? They were too busy with their new plays and precious costumes.

Kit took a deep breath. *Phew!* The ripe smell of garbage and manure struck him. He had been in the green fields of Shoreditch for a week, long enough to forget the powerful stink of London. His nose would get used to it soon enough, but what of his growling stomach? He had not had his dinner. He slipped into Cornhill Street, filled with stalls selling oysters, cheese, cakes, pudding, and all sorts of good things to eat.

"Pies! Meat pies!" called a woman. Kit stopped at her stall and sniffed. "What will it be, lad? Pork or pigeon?"

"I have no money," said Kit.

"Off with you then," said the woman. "You stand in the way of customers."

Kit found the bread man who sometimes gave him a leftover loaf.

"Come back later," the man said. "I am still selling."

A fishmonger chopped heads off salmon. Slow autumn flies buzzed around the pail. Roger made a good soup from fish heads and turnips. Maybe...

"Might I have those, if you please?" asked Kit.

The fishmonger went on chopping. "Why should I give them away, when I might sell them for —?" He looked at Kit, and his face softened. "Very well, but you cannot take the bucket."

Why had the man changed his mind? True, Kit looked ill-dressed for November. Whatever the reason, he was glad of it. He wrapped the fish heads in a rag, and the flies followed him as he left the market, heading through the lanes toward the river.

When he reached a dilapidated warehouse, he shouted the old signal. "Bolts and shackles! Fire and brimstone!" Two boys appeared at the doorway, but Kit did not know them. One had ginger hair. The other sprouted big ears that stuck straight out from his head.

"Who are you?" Ginger asked.

"Who are *you*?" Kit replied. "Where is Roger?"

"Who wants to know?"

"I do — Roger's mate."

The two young boys looked at each other. "We know you not," Big Ears said.

"I know you not either. How long have you been here?"

Ginger shrugged. "Some days now," he said.

"Where is Roger?" Kit repeated.

"He be sleeping."

Roger worked at night, outside the taverns when drunken men could not see him or feel the touch of the knife cutting their purses. Kit held out the rag filled with fish heads and walked toward the door. "I have got me something for his supper."

The boys backed up against the door. "We cannot let strangers pass."

"I am not a stranger. I be his mate, I told you."

"What is all the racket then?" Roger stood in the doorway, squinting. When he saw Kit, he exclaimed, "Hoy-day! The clumsiest blockhead in London. You got some brass to come here, you do."

Kit shifted from one foot to the other. "I nipped me two bungs without being caught. Then..."

Roger walked toward Kit. "I saw the whole botched bungle." He threw back his head. "Ha! That be your right name. Kit Bungles!"

Ginger and Big Ears joined in laughing.

Kit was too stunned to reply.

"What does it matter how many bungs you nipped? How much money did you bring me?"

"Nought."

Roger took a step toward Kit. "So what have you to brag about?"

"Nought." Kit took a step backward.

"Why do you poke around here?" Roger raised his fist.

Kit looked beyond the fist into Roger's blue eyes. "They kept me prisoner at the playhouse, and I only escaped just now. I want to come back."

Roger peered down the alley. "Did anyone follow you?"

"No."

"Then run away the same way you came!" he shouted.

Kit held out his dripping rag. "But Roger, I brought you some fish heads for supper."

"Fish heads! You think I want your stinking fish heads?" He spat on the ground.

"For soup..." Kit dropped his arms.

"Stow you!" Roger snarled as he moved toward Kit. "Your first day in the playhouse and you got caught." Kit stepped backward and slipped on the cobblestones. "You did raise such a riot that every rogue, including the ones on the stage, saw your ugly mug."

Kit stumbled away from Roger.

"One thousand joltheads did see that Kit Bungles is a dimwitted oaf with fingers like big toes when it comes to nipping a bung. And worse than that, none of us dare to go near the playhouse now. That money-gatherer has an eagle eye out for coves who want to do what you could not."

Kit backed into a wall, but Roger kept coming closer. "And a wench did bring you down. A miserable wench!"

"I'm most grievous sorry." Kit could think of nothing more to say.

Roger was nearly nose-to-nose with him. He spat again, spraying Kit's boots. "So take your clumsy carcass and them stinking fish heads where I cannot smell you. And come not running to me anymore." He cracked his knuckles. "If ever I see you round here again, you will be more than 'most grievous sorry.' Do you hear?"

"Yes, Roger."

Roger walked back inside and slammed the door.

Kit felt a wave of anger crash over him. He lifted the fish heads to hurl at the door, then paused. He had seen Roger fight with his fists and feet and even his head, jamming it into an unguarded belly.

"You heard him. Get you gone." Ginger and Big Ears picked up clods of dirt and flung them at Kit.

He jumped aside. "Why you bawling brats!" Kit cried. He ran toward the boys swinging the fishy rag.

"Roger, Roger, he's coming back!" the two boys yelled.

The door banged open and Roger appeared, his face twisted with rage. Kit took off down the alley, turned a corner, and kept running. Finally, slowed by a crowd of people coming from the market, he ducked into a side lane. He chucked the fish heads in the gutter, in with the horse manure that clogged the filthy water streaming down the lane.

An orange cat jumped from a windowsill to snatch the fish heads. A speckled dog, so skinny its ribs poked out, ran up and tried to do the same. The dog barked and lunged for the fish. The cat hissed and lashed out at the dog.

A woman came to a doorway and threw a stone at them. "Away with you!" she yelled.

With a yowl and a growl, the cat and dog scampered away.

Kit walked on, his shoulders hunched, his eyes on the ground, stepping over garbage rotting in puddles. A flock of honking geese suddenly surrounded Kit. One bold goose nipped the back of Kit's leg, and he stumbled. The boy leading the flock laughed. Kit clenched his fists and lurched forward. But surrounded by waddling geese, he could not move. When the flock had passed, he remained standing in the middle of the street.

His stomach hurt, and he pressed a fist into his belly. He had eaten nothing since breakfast. The bread man would be gone now, the market empty. London Bridge lay ahead, with the dreadful heads on stakes, blackened with tar, eyes picked out by ravens. Kit shuddered. He had to find a place to sleep, but not by the river where those heads would give him nightmares.

As he turned back from the bridge, a man carrying a basket hit him hard in the shoulder. Kit raised his hand to rub his shoulder, and his elbow jabbed a woman holding a baby.

"Clumsy Jack-sauce," she snapped as the baby began to cry.

Kit shrank from her and snaked through the crowds. His shoulder hurt, and his feet ached. Finally he reached the broad avenue of Cheapside. A butcher was locking his doors for the night, so Kit sat down on the shop steps. The butcher frowned and came back to check that the shutters were secure. He gave Kit a wary glance and said, "I know your lot."

Kit was too exhausted to feel angry. He stretched out his legs and wiggled his toes. His old brown boots were getting tight. Where would he get his next pair? He rubbed his sore shoulder. He could not sleep here on the butcher's doorstep. The night watchmen would make him move on. Gangs of apprentices might beat him for sport. He could rest a few minutes though, and so he leaned against the door and closed his eyes.

ACT SECOND, SCENE II

Shadow

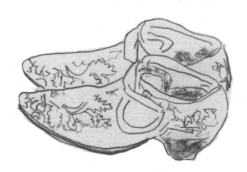

Kit's eyes popped open. What was that? Someone hummed a song he knew. Kit peered into the shadowy street, but he could not see who it was.

Then a man began to sing:

"When that I was a little tiny boy,
With a heigh ho, the wind and the rain
A foolish thing was but a toy
For the rain it raineth every day."

As the singer passed, Kit recognized Will Shakespeare. He sat up. Did Mr. Shakespeare know he had run away? He had been kind to Kit before. Perhaps he would help him now. Then Kit slumped back against the doorway, remembering the last angry look Mr. Shakespeare had given him after his fight with Nicholas.

With a heigh ho, the wind and the rain. . . . .

The song drew Kit to his feet as if by a magic spell. He followed Will Shakespeare like a shadow, careful to stay out of sight. Mr. Shakespeare ambled down the middle of the street. People and even a raucous bunch of pigs gave way for him. Kit pressed against a wall as the pigs trotted past. Then, stepping over pig droppings, he hurried to keep Mr. Shakespeare in sight.

He had warned Kit not to go back to Roger. He had been right. He had told him to work hard. 'Twas easy to say, harder to do. A woman emptied a chamber pot out of an upstairs window, splashing Kit's boots. He leaped forward, turned a corner, and saw Mr. Shakespeare walking past St. Paul's Cathedral.

A voice called out above the din of the crowd, "Ballads, my master, ballads. Will you have o' the newest and truest matter in all London?"

Kit hid behind a tree and watched Mr. Shakespeare browse among the bookstalls on the far side of the cathedral.

Another seller shouted, "Fine ballads! New ballads! Here be your story-ballads, your love ballads, and your ballads of good life!" He greeted Will Shakespeare like an old friend and handed him his wares. Mr. Shakespeare studied each ballad. Finally he bought two, handing over two pennies.

Kit had heard ballads sung in the marketplace. He had read them pasted on tavern walls. They told of confessions of evil witches, robberies by ruthless highwaymen, or bloody murders here in London. Once Kit had read about a monstrous fish caught off the coast of Holland. The lines Will Shakespeare wrote were far better than the ballad verses, so why did he buy them?

Kit watched Mr. Shakespeare wander from stall to stall. When he walked back toward Bishopsgate, Kit stayed several yards behind him. The sky overhead held a bit of light, but none of it made its way to the dark street, and Kit stumbled over ruts in the road. Mr. Shakespeare had stopped singing now, and only muffled sounds came from within the houses as women called their families to supper. Shutters were clapped shut against the dangers of the night.

Will Shakespeare stopped outside a house near the city wall. He looked up and down the street, and Kit slid into an alley. Mr. Shakespeare unlocked the door and stepped into the house. The windows had bars across them, to keep thieving boys from crawling in and stealing the silver.

Kit made his way to the end of the alley, pulled his doublet close, leaned against a wall, and slid to the ground. He knew not where he would go tomorrow or when he would eat, but he was too tired to think of it now. He closed his eyes, but sleep did not come. He felt the cold stones bite into his back. He had slept outside last August when he first came to London, but it was warm then. A cold drizzle wet his face now. Winter was closing in. "The rain it raineth every day" was the right song for this time of year.

Last winter he had slept in a drafty farm cottage loft. After Grannie and Grandsire died, a farmer had given him a home of sorts, not out of kindness, but to work him like a slave. Kit had spread wet, stinking dung on the fields in the spring; weeded the fields and scared birds away from the growing grain in the hot summer sun; and bound endless sheaves of barley that cut and blistered his hands. Farmwork was hard, but that was not the worst of it. It made him beef-brained, as dull as the cows he milked each day.

Kit remembered his grandsire singing as he worked in the shipyard. His father had spun tales of fighting the wind and waves at sea, and of pirates too. But Kit sang no songs and spun no tales on the farm. The thought of working as a hired hand all his life had made him duller still.

Folks told stories of London where a boy could find adventure, learn a trade, make a fortune. When the farmer drove his cattle to the city to sell, he had taken Kit along to help. But when they reached London, Kit had slipped away, sleeping in the fields until he reckoned the farmer had gone home again.

London had frightened him at first, but the crowds and teeming markets excited him, too. He was determined to make his way. The days on his own until Roger took him in, then the weeks with Roger seemed a long-ago dream now as he huddled in the cold, damp alley.

When he learned that Roger meant him for a cutpurse, Kit had protested. He did not want to become a thief. But Roger fed him and gave him a patch of straw to sleep on, out of the rain. Besides, Roger said, people had so much money in London! What were a few nipped bungs?

Kit shivered, too cold to fall asleep. It was pitch dark now. He heard the watchmen in the distance, making their rounds. "Ho, watchmen, ho. Look well to your lock, your fire, and your light."

He heard footsteps stumble down the street, then enter the alley. The footsteps stopped and he heard a man groan as he relieved himself. Kit held his breath. No respectable men walked the streets this late at night. He had nothing for anyone to steal, but he might be murdered for no reason at all. When the footsteps moved away, Kit let out his breath.

Where could he go? What could he do? His father had meant for him to go to sea. His grandsire had talked of apprenticing him to a shipwright. Now his father and his grandsire were dead. He would not go back to the farm, and he could not join Roger's gang again. He had thrown away his chance at the playhouse. What would be his fate? Kit put his head on his knees. At last, hungry and cold and weary beyond measure, he dropped into sleep.

Pityhound

Kit awoke hungry, thirsty, and sore. His neck hurt. His back ached. It was dark in the alley, but when he entered the street, people were stirring. If he got to the market now, he could help the sellers set up their stalls.

Carts rumbled down Cheapside. Beating hammers and clinking pots filled the early morning air. Even louder were the men and women already hawking their wares.

"New fresh herring!"

"Hot cockles!"

"Ripe chestnuts, walnuts, and small nuts!"

"What do you lack? What lack you?"

"Buy any ink; very fine pens!"

"Garlic and gooseberries!"

"Fine shirts and smocks!"

"Very fine combs and glasses!"

"Have you corns on your toes?"

"Brooms, brooms!"

"What do you lack?"

Another day began in London.

Kit unloaded barrels of wine from a wine-seller's cart and wooden toys for a toy-maker. He earned a penny and spent it on a loaf of bread. He pushed a handcart of secondhand clothes and traded his labor for a woolen hat.

He was arranging a pile of apples in a pyramid on a rickety stall when someone said, "How now! 'Tis the runaway, Kit Buckles. Mercy, mercy! You be a sorry sight."

Kit whirled around to see Molly, standing with one hand on her hip and a basket on her arm. "What brings you here?" he demanded.

"The same what brings me here every morning. I come for apples for the afternoon play. 'Tis a better question — what brings you here? You should have heard Tom yesterday, when he found you did not clean the ground. I am surprised his curses did not set the thatch roof on fire." She laughed a long, musical laugh.

Kit frowned. "I could bear it no longer."

"Bear it? To work for your living?"

Kit glared at her. "I could not bear Tom's sneering and Nicholas's high and mighty attitude."

The apple seller said, "Choose you your apples, love, and chat you with your lad somewhere else." She handed Kit two apples. "'Tis for your help."

While Molly chose her apples, Kit ate one of his. He looked hungrily at the second one, but he did not know when he would get more to eat. He put the apple inside his doublet.

"You are hungry," she said.

"No," lied Kit.

"Come," Molly said, tugging on his sleeve.

Kit leaned away from her, but she pulled harder and led him behind the apple stall.

"You are the most stubborn boy that ever I knew!"

"I am not as stubborn as Nicholas."

"You are worse, much worse!"

Kit ducked his head to hide a smile. "If I am, what of it?"

"You be twelve, my own age, but you act like a peevish child. Sit you down." She pushed him onto an apple box and sat beside him. Molly sniffed. "My eyes, where slept you last night — a dung heap?"

Kit looked at his filthy clothes. He brushed them off and caught a whiff of rotten fish. "'Tis my business and none of yours."

"Do you want to sleep there again tonight?"

"'Tis not for you to know."

Molly sighed. "As you will. I will ask no more questions. Well, just one, and answer you this. Would you come back to the playhouse?"

Kit cocked his head. "Would they take me back?"

She slapped the box she sat on. "'Tis not an answer!"

Kit dragged his toe in the mud. The playhouse was his best chance, his only chance. "Maybe I would return. But why do you help me?"

"Do I? I want to help the players. We have got troubles, which you would know, if you were not so fixed on your own. You are like to a pitiful hound, ears dragging in the dirt. A pityhound, 'tis what you are." She giggled.

Kit kicked an apple core into the gutter. "What know you of my troubles?"

Molly counted them on her fingers. "I know that you are an orphan, you got a bad start in London, you had a chance to mend your ways; but you pick fights and feel sorry for yourself instead, and now you are back on the street."

Kit wrenched his cap off his head and twirled it furiously around his fist. "'Tis easy for you. You have no troubles."

Molly jumped up from her apple box and nearly upset her basket. Kit grabbed for the basket, but Molly was quicker. She set it down again and thrust out her arm at Kit. "No troubles? Look you here. See this hand, how 'twill not go straight?"

Kit stared at her crooked hand. He had not noticed it before.

"One night — I was but six years old — my dad came home drunk as usual and started beating Mam. I tried to beat him, but he picked me up by my wrist and threw me across the room like a sack of flour." Molly glanced at her hand, still pointing at Kit. "He pulled things apart in my wrist, and they never healed right."

Kit stared at her hand. "Does it hurt you?"

She looked up at the lowering sky. "Only when it rains." She raised her chin. "I was glad when Dad disappeared for good. But Mam never had food enough for us — me and two little ones. So when I was eight, she sent me out to work. I have got scars in places I will not show you from the whippings I got because I was too clumsy or too slow."

Molly began pacing back and forth. "Once the fire smoked and left coal dust on my mistress's precious china cats. She made me sleep in the coal hole to see how I liked being covered in coal dust. A rat bit me, and I got the fever and nearly died. Not that my mistress cared. When I was well again, she put me out on the street; but my next place was as bad as the first. After two years of whippings, my uncle met a man who knew Tom; and I got my job at the playhouse and a bed with Mr. Richard's family."

Kit could think of nothing to say. Finally he offered, "At least you have got good luck now."

Molly stamped her foot. "'Tis not luck, Kit Buckles," she cried as she slapped her chest. "Molly Godden is honest, and she works hard every day." She picked up her basket. "And I do not grumble and run if things do not go my way."

She plucked an apple from her basket with her good hand and rubbed it against her skirt so hard that Kit thought she would rub the skin off. "Do you think that you are the only one with troubles? Look at the people in Mr. Shakespeare's plays. His princesses have cruel fathers. Their mothers die. Little princes are murdered. And if that be not bad enough, look you to our Queen Elizabeth. Her best friends and her own cousin, Scottish Queen Mary, plot to kill her and take her crown."

Molly's voice got more and more shrill, until Kit was certain the whole of Cheapside Market could hear her. If she were a boy, she could be on the stage. "No one will save you from hard times, Kit. But no one wants to kill you, do they?" She pointed her crooked hand at Kit. "Do they?"

Kit thought of Roger. "To beat me, perhaps...."

"Then you are luckier than our queen." She folded her arms across her chest and gave him a haughty look.

Luckier than the queen? Kit knew not how to answer. He felt as stupid as an old boot. He reached into his doublet for his apple and took a bite. "What is wrong at the playhouse? Crowds of people come every day and pay their pennies," he said.

"That is not the problem. Years ago James Burbage, Mr. Richard's father, built the Theatre on Giles Allen's land. He paid rent for the land, but now Mr. Allen wants to lock them out of the building."

"Why?" asked Kit, dragging his toe in the mud again.

"I am not certain."

"'Tis not fair if they built the playhouse."

Molly raised her eyebrows. "And if 'twere not enough, they are one apprentice short. He took ill and left last month."

Kit saw that he had drawn the shape of the playhouse in the dirt with his toe. Now he drew the outline of the stage in the middle.

Molly continued. "But I know not if they would trust you even to clean the muck off the ground, after your runaway yesterday. Do you dare to ask?"

Did he? Rain began to trickle down his neck. He pulled his shirt collar up. The weather would drive people from the market, and he would get no more work or food today. The thought of sleeping in the rain tonight made him shiver.

"I must needs go back," said Molly. She picked up her basket of apples and set off down the street.

Kit watched her go. Should he fling off his pride and ask to be taken back? Could he choke down such a big hunk of humble pie? His stomach rumbled. The rain fell harder as Kit jumped up and ran after Molly.

Messenger

"Who should I ask about coming back?" Kit asked Molly when he caught up with her.

"Mr. Burbage."

"He wants to give me to the sheriff!" exclaimed Kit.

"Not Richard. His brother, Cuthbert. 'Tis he who takes charge of the business of the playhouse. You will find him up in the attic."

"I would rather ask Mr. Shakespeare," said Kit.

Molly shook her head. "Do not bother him. His head is full of plots and poetry and such."

Tom stood at the door the playhouse. "You!" he yelled and shook his fist at Kit. "Dare you to show your face here?"

Kit ducked past him and began to climb the stairs to the attic. On the landing, he bumped into Mr. Shakespeare. "Pray pardon, sir," he said.

Mr. Shakespeare threw his hands into the air. "You did come back!"

Kit bowed his head and mumbled, "I have nowhere else to go."

"Is that a good reason to return?"

Kit looked up and saw Mr. Shakespeare's eyes boring into him. Kit took a deep breath and let it out again. Confusion filled his head like fog on a marsh at dawn.

Will Shakespeare winked. "Boys with spirit make mistakes. If they are lucky, they live to become men with spirit, but they do not stop making mistakes."

Kit kept silent.

"Why did you follow me to the bookstalls yesterday?" Mr. Shakespeare had a sly smile on his face.

Startled, Kit replied, "Why did you buy common broadsheets instead of fine books?"

Mr. Shakespeare laughed. "Why not? Everything is food for my plays. Pretty poems in books, dreadful news of the day, even boys shadowing me. I savor it all."

His smile gave Kit courage. "Would you let me work again at the playhouse, sir? I will not fight, and I will do whatever you ask."

"I am not in charge, Kit. I am just a hired scribbler." He nodded toward the attic. "Cuthbert is the man to ask."

"But he knows me not. Could you speak to him for me?"

"No, I could not," said Will Shakespeare. " 'Tis your task. 'Tis mine to finish Act II by tomorrow, and then to begin Act III. King Henry V calls me, or at least his story does."

He grabbed Kit's elbows and danced him around the narrow landing. Kit stumbled.

"You are writing a play too, lad, the play of your life, with all the world as your stage. Act I, or perhaps Act II, is about to begin. Will it be a comedy or a tragedy? 'Tis your choice. Whatever it be, leap into it, dance with it. Listen for the rhythm, find the tune, and dance!" He laughed and twirled Kit round.

Kit, dizzy and astonished, stared at Will Shakespeare.

Shakespeare imitated Tom's gruff voice. "You do as I tell you, lad!" Then he skipped down the stairs. He turned, looked up at Kit, and snapped his fingers. "Dance!"

Dance with his life? On the stage of the world? Sometimes Mr. Shakespeare's words made good sense and sometimes they seemed as murky as the water in the River Thames.

Upstairs he heard voices. Mr. Richard boomed, others murmured. He could sneak away now, and no one would miss him. Or he could climb the stairs and try to write the next scene for himself, here at the playhouse. Molly walked by downstairs but didn't see him. She was brave. Was he? He stood there a minute longer. Then he climbed the stairs and knocked on the door, his heart knocking nearly as loud.

Molly sat on the edge of the stage as Kit emptied a sack of nutshells. They kept the ground from turning to mud or dust, depending on the weather.

"How did you fare?" Molly asked.

Kit raked the shells smooth. "I asked Mr. Cuthbert's pardon for fighting and running away. I told him I wished to show him I was honest and hardworking."

Kit did not tell Molly how his knees shook and his voice, too — so much that he had to repeat his words twice before Mr. Cuthbert understood him. Kit went on raking nutshells. "I said I was most sorry for his troubles and did not want to add to them. Mr. Richard made a queer noise and looked daggers at me." Kit had wanted to run out the door then, but he did not say that to Molly.

"Mr. Cuthbert said they needed every hand in these hard times, and he would give me a trial for a week. If Tom gave me a good report, I could stay for another week, and then another. Mr. Cuthbert asked if I knew my way through the city. I said I could find my way blindfolded, just from the smells." Everyone in the room had laughed at that, even Mr. Richard. Now Molly laughed.

Kit went on. "Mr. Cuthbert said he needed a messenger boy, but he wanted a good report from Tom first."

Molly pointed to the ground behind Kit. "You need more nutshells back there."

Kit frowned. Must he take orders from Molly too? He sneaked a look at her as she examined his work. Was she friend or foe? She did like to speak her mind and tell him what to do. And she was cleverer than he was. Well, he would not fret about Molly, but do what he must to stay here with the players.

In the days to come, Kit often thought of Mr. Shakespeare dancing on the stairs. It helped him ignore Nicholas's rude comments and

Tom's grumbles. Kit skipped a bit while he swept the stage, if no one was about. He even sang a song he had heard James sing.

"Three merry men and three merry men and
Three merry men are we.
I in the wood, and you on the ground,
And Jack sleeps in the tree."

Until Tom yelled, "Stop you that howling!"

A week later Mr. Cuthbert sent for Kit. "Tom tells me your work is no worse than he expected. Coming from Tom, 'tis a right good report. Will Shakespeare said that your dancing feet help you sweep the stage faster than ever."

Kit blushed. "He saw me?"

"Will sees more than any of us. But enough praise. 'Twill swell your head." Mr. Cuthbert shuffled through a pile of papers on his desk and drew one out. "I want you to deliver this letter to the George Inn in Southwark. Know you the way?"

Kit nodded. "Down Shoreditch to Bishopsgate, straight on to London Bridge, across the bridge, then past St. Mary's Church but before the market." Roger had made his boys learn the maze of streets and lanes in the city, to better escape from their victims.

"You do know the city well. Give this letter to Master Peter Street, or to the innkeeper, if Peter be not there." Mr. Cuthbert took a stick of wax and lit it. When a drop of liquid wax fell on the letter, he pressed it with his ring to make a seal.

"No one must see this but Master Street or the innkeeper. We are on a secret course, Kit. You will learn more of it soon." He handed the letter to Kit. "Now run, or even dance, if 'twill get you there faster."

Kit darted among the crowds at Bishopsgate. London Bridge was so jammed with carts and people that he slowed to a walk. He put the letter inside his shirt, and twice a minute he patted his chest to make sure it was safe. When he got to the inn and announced his mission, the woman behind the bar held out her hand.

" 'Tis a private letter for Master Street," Kit said.

The barmaid sniffed. "And who be you, the queen's own messenger?"

"By your leave, madam." Kit pressed his hand against his shirt.

She thrust her chin toward a back room.

Kit entered and saw a crowd of men at a long table, finishing their dinner of beef and ale.

All eyes rested on a small brown-haired man telling a story. He had a high voice and cocked his head from side to side. When he got to the end of the tale, a roar of laughter rolled around the table. But the chittering laugh of the storyteller rose above it all. He picked up his beef in two hands and took quick bites. Kit walked over to him and held out the letter. "Master Street?"

More laughter rang out.

"Oh, so you be the master now, Samuel?"

"Heaven help us!"

Samuel's chitter rose above the noise. "Oh no, oh dear no, I am not Master Street."

Kit blushed crimson and looked round the table. A tall black-haired man rose from a bench.

"I'll take that."

"Are you Master Street?" Kit held back the letter.

"I am."

Samuel called, " 'Tis he, laddie. 'Tis he and no one else."

Kit handed Peter Street the letter. "I mean no disrespect, sir. Mr. Cuthbert did insist I hand it to you."

Peter Street broke open the wax seal on the letter and read it quickly. "Tell Cuthbert I will come to see him tomorrow at eight in the morning."

Mr. Cuthbert was surprised to see Kit return so soon. "You must have Mercury's wings on your feet."

"Sir?"

"Mercury, the messenger of the gods. Since he does not work here, we will use you as our runner instead." He chuckled at his own joke.

Kit smiled and said, "I thank you, sir."

ACT SECOND, SCENE V

Soldier

"They need another soldier in Act Three," Tom barked.

Kit opened a trunk to search for a helmet and cloak. Tom shook his head. "They need a soldier, not just a costume. A hired man did not come today. You will have to do."

Kit stared. "I, a player?"

"You will not be important — just a body to fill up the space. You are a bit short, but we take us what we got. Stand you at the back, march you with the rest, and shout 'hurrah' when they do. Then raise your shield and march you off again."

Kit hurried to put on his costume. He followed two soldiers

onstage, bumped into one, started his hurrah a little late, and nearly tripped Nicholas as he left the stage.

"I played a soldier onstage today," Kit told Molly after the play.

"Did it please you?"

He paused to consider. "I was too uneasy to notice."

"I will watch for you next time," Molly said.

Next time? Molly had told him that an apprentice player had left. Might he take his place? But no one spoke about another apprentice, and no chance came to play another soldier. And so he kept on with cleaning the ground and washing the bloody shirts.

Every day rumors flew through the playhouse like bats through the summer night sky.

"Mr. Cuthbert said he will burn down the playhouse rather than give it to Mr. Allen."

"Will Shakespeare threatens to quit writing plays and write only poetry instead."

"Mr. Richard has challenged Giles Allen to a duel!"

Kit understood little of it. He was on the streets nearly every day, taking and collecting messages for Mr. Cuthbert. It was early December now, and fewer people came to the playhouse on cold, rainy afternoons.

One morning Mr. Cuthbert called the whole company together. "You know we are having a legal dispute with Giles Allen. He refuses to renew the lease for the playhouse." He held up his hand. "I misspeak. The lease for the land *beneath* the playhouse. As you know, the playhouse itself is ours, *not* Allen's. He claims that we are trespassing here, that he owns the building now that the lease has expired. I received a final notice from his lawyer this morning and learned that the sheriff will lock us out of our — I repeat — *our* playhouse at midnight tonight."

A roar of protests interrupted Mr. Cuthbert. He raised his voice. "We knew this might happen, but we knew not when. I have cancelled the play this afternoon. Everyone must help to move us to the Curtain playhouse down the road. 'Tis without a company of players now, and we shall lease it until this feud is settled. Have no fear. Though we beat a temporary retreat, we do not surrender! You may have heard some wild rumors, but pay them no mind. We will win back our playhouse!" Cuthbert thrust his fist into the air, and the players cheered.

Mr. Cuthbert went on. "Giles Allen is evicting us now, but he will get nothing — not an ink bottle, not a pin — that we can carry away. We have sixteen hours until midnight. Get you to work, men!"

Chaos reigned for the rest of the day. People shouted questions, orders, and all sorts of rude language. Some of the stage properties refused to fit round the corners and out the doors. Men carrying crates of costumes bumped into other men toting boxes of papers. Thumps and crashes echoed through the building.

Kit carried boxes up from the cellar and down from the attic. He loaded carts and ran to the Curtain playhouse where he unloaded carts, carried boxes upstairs and down, then moved them somewhere else. Molly brought bread, cheese, and apples for the workers, but Kit barely had time to take a bite before he was called to work again. He felt excited and fearful, anxious and giddy. The day was filled with suspense, just like a play, and he knew not how it would end.

When the church bells chimed 11:45 that night, the sheriff and two of his men arrived at the Theatre with lock and chain. Kit was coiling a length of rope outside the doorway.

Mr. Richard thundered, "You will not lock us out yet. Stand aside." He pushed past one of the sheriff's men and entered the playhouse one last time. The man moved to stop him, but the sheriff held up his hand. At the first toll of the bells at midnight, the sheriff chained the doors and attached a huge iron lock. He began to read, "By order of the High Sheriff and the undersigned Lessor —"

"Waste not your breath, sir," said Mr. Richard. "Come, Chamberlain's Men, we have work to do."

The sheriff stood with his mouth open as Mr. Richard and the others marched past him with the last cartload of properties. Kit held his coiled rope before him like a soldier's shield. The players had retreated with dignity, and he felt proud to be part of their army.

ACT SECOND, SCENE VI

Lady's Maid

The company began performing at the Curtain three days later.

"We have higher rent to pay here, but the we must carry on, or our audience will forsake us for another company," Mr. Cuthbert told Kit as he handed him a letter for their new landlord.

During the first week, the players did little but complain.

"'Tis the wrong doublet!"

"Where is my old rapier?"

"The stage is so small I nearly stepped off the edge today."

Kit unpacked the costumes and tried to set them in order. He watched the stage crew cut down some of the stage properties to fit the new space, and helped to build a bonfire with the wood scraps left over. And he still delivered messages for Mr. Cuthbert.

"I know more about this playhouse drama than anyone else," Kit boasted to Molly one morning as he set out costumes.

"You dare not read the letters you deliver!" Molly cried.

Her accusation stung him. "Of course not," he snapped. "Mr. Cuthbert puts his seal on each one. But he drops a few words, and other people drop a few more, and I put them all together."

Kit fell silent and spread the full skirt of Nicholas's gown. He was learning a thing or two about playing a part. In a moment of silence, the audience leans forward and marks well the player.

"Tell me!" cried Molly.

Kit puffed up the sleeves and kept still. He liked an eager audience, even an audience of one. Especially one who was always so keen to put him in his place. Finally he said, "Mr. Allen refuses to take the lock off the door, and Mr. Cuthbert refuses to give the building to Mr. Allen."

Molly waved her hand. "Everyone knows that!"

Kit held up his own hand. "Wait," he said. "Both sides have lawyers that do nothing but trade insults with each other and charge Mr. Cuthbert a fortune for something he could do face-to-face in half a minute."

Molly sighed impatiently, but Kit was the leading player in this scene.

He sat down on a stool and leaned back against the table. "There is a gentleman across the river, who sends big packets of papers to Mr. Cuthbert and his lawyer." He leaned forward. "I even took a letter to the Bishop of Winchester's palace in Southwark. If you could see it, Molly. 'Tis as grand as a queen's palace, I trow."

"What has Mr. Cuthbert to do with the bishop?"

Kit scowled. "Southwark is full of gambling dens and other evil places. There's a bear-baiting pit, where poor old bears and fierce dogs try to kill each other."

Molly shuddered.

Kit went on. "The bishop owns those dreadful places, or at least collects fees from the people who own them."

"The bishop approves of that sort of thing?"

Kit shrugged. "He approves of the money it brings him."

"What has all this got to do with us?" Molly asked.

"My guess is that Mr. Cuthbert wants to move us to Southwark." He crossed his arms. Molly's eyes were wide, like a groundling carried away by a scene on the stage.

"To which playhouse?"

"The Rose and the Swan are both in Southwark, but they have their own companies of players." Kit screwed up his face. "'Tis the piece of the puzzle I have not found yet. But I know for certain that Mr. Cuthbert has a plan."

Molly laughed. "Kit Buckles, Master Spy. You might have a future at the Queen's court."

The spell was broken. Molly was mocking him again. Could he not even tell a story without her jeering? Master Spy, Queen's court. Though they were the same in years, she made him feel young and foolish — a right ninnyhammer. Just one of hundreds of hapless boys crisscrossing London, carrying messages for more worthy people.

Boys not lucky enough or rich enough to buy an apprenticeship, to have a master and a future. Kit slumped on the stool. He was but a rootless lad with no future at all, and he could not even have a little fun without Molly reminding him of that. He stood, kicked the stool over, and left the room.

"Why are you . . . ?" he heard her call.

The next day they wanted Kit onstage again. He played a lady's maid. The folks in Suffolk might hoot with laughter, but London playgoers knew that boys were meant to play girls' roles. Kit fancied himself a Londoner now, not a rude country lout.

It took James a quarter of an hour to teach him how to walk like a girl — straight on with small steps, not swaying side to side. Kit was to say, "Yes, my lady"; then, "Come away, my lady"; and then, "Yes, my lady," once more.

During the play he was so wary of tripping on his dress that he hardly noticed the audience till he heard someone shout, "What a lovely wench you are, little maid! Would you like to come home with me?"

Kit froze, but James, playing the lady, looked at Kit and said, "Methinks I hear a crow squawking. Do you hear it?"

The audience burst out laughing. Kit struggled not to laugh with them. He dropped his gaze as a shy maid would do. This was a right frolic!

After the play, Molly said, "Your first 'my lady' sounded like a street-seller, and the second I could not hear; but the third time you got it right."

Kit scowled. "If you think 'tis so easy, then you try it."

"I did not mean to —"

But Kit stomped away.

In the days that followed, Kit shadowed Nicholas and James. He spied on their rapier practice, music lessons, and rehearsals. If no one was about, he would slash his broom through the air like a swordsman.

"Come you here, Kit," said Mr. Phillips, the music master, one morning. "We need another dancer this afternoon." Kit lived with kind Mr. Phillips and had seen him play on the stage, but he had never chosen Kit for a dancer.

"Do not dress him as a girl. He will trip on his gown," said Nicholas.

Several people laughed, but Mr. Phillips frowned. "When I want your counsel, Nicholas, I will ask for it." The laughter stopped.

Kit quickly learned the steps. He was pleased to see Nicholas stumble several times. Mr. Phillips asked, "What troubles you, Nicholas? You did dance this dance a dozen times."

"My slippers are too tight," he muttered.

"Curl your toes under, or find yourself another pair," ordered Mr. Phillips.

Kit hid a smile. He knew the company owned no ladies' slippers larger than the ones Nicholas wore. Perhaps Kit himself would wear those shoes someday.

Kit took his place onstage at the end of the play, dressed as a boy. Will Kemp, the clown, cavorted about, bawling out rude jokes and songs. Mr. Shakespeare hated such jigs. He said they destroyed the mood of his play, and sent the audience home with coarse songs in their heads, not his fine lines.

But people loved Will Kemp. They laughed and hollered, especially when he leaped to the front of the stage and tossed jests and insults to the groundlings. They took his taunts, twisted them, and tossed them back to him. Finally Will Kemp signaled for the dance to begin.

Kit stepped back and forth, skipping and twirling, never taking his eyes off his partners. He felt as well-tuned as the lute that played for the dance. When it was over, he lined up with the other dancers and made a deep bow. The audience whistled and clapped, and Kit gazed at the hundreds of people before him. Dancing had been pleasure enough. To please the crowd and hear their applause were added thrills.

The dancers stepped back as the players came forward. Nicholas stepped to the front, and the clapping grew louder. He took hold of his wide skirts and made a deep curtsey. Mr. Richard came onstage, and people began to whistle and shout.

Kit looked out at the playhouse. It was only half full today, but the applause seemed to fill the sky. Might the audience clap just for him one day? If the company needed a player's apprentice, as Molly said, they could have Kit Buckles. For the first time since he arrived in London, he saw a path into his future. Mr. Shakespeare had said the whole world was his stage. Perhaps the stage might become his whole world, the place where he belonged.

Stage Boy

Next morning Mr. Cuthbert announced to the company, "The Queen has invited us to perform twice at Whitehall Palace after Christmas."

Excited talk filled the stage.

"We will not freeze this Christmastide," said James.

"Why not?" asked Kit.

"The Master of the Revels must approve our play before we perform for the queen, to see that we say nothing wrong."

"What would that be?" asked Kit.

"Any lines that make kings and queens appear immoral or foolish. Any story about good people plotting against evil royals. So we rehearse in the Hall of Revels where the Master can watch us. They have coal fires blazing in every room, and they give us right plentiful food and hot drinks too. 'Tis a fair sight better than this place," James said, shivering as freezing rain poured out of the sky.

Kit's heart did a hop and a skip. Surely they would need extra players to play for the Queen. When he left Suffolk last summer, he never imagined he would meet Queen Elizabeth by the New Year. He must talk to Mr. Shakespeare about becoming a player's apprentice.

The next day Kit saw Will Shakespeare pacing back and forth across the stage. Kit walked toward him, but Mr. Shakespeare walked past, so close he nearly brushed Kit's arm, then turned on his heels and paced back again. Kit crept away. Mr. Shakespeare was lost in his imagination.

Next day and the day after that, Mr. Shakespeare arrived at the playhouse surrounded by Mr. Richard and the players. They rehearsed one scene after another. Then they argued and shouted. Kit had never seen Mr. Shakespeare so agitated. 'Twas not the time to talk to him. Meanwhile every dress and doublet had to be cleaned and mended. Tom gave the orders, and Kit and James did most of the work. James was an expert with a needle, and Kit polished all the boots and washed the doublets.

"The Queen fancies herself an expert on plays and players, and tells us when we do not please her," said James. "She is paying us ten pounds, and she wants her money's worth!"

"Zounds!" exclaimed Kit "Ten pounds! That should help pay our rent."

James shrugged. "Perhaps. We will need us some new costumes and properties to dazzle the royal eyes. The audience sits close enough to notice any peeling paint or stained coat. Everything must be perfect."

"They should replace this old cloak," said Kit, plunging it into a tub of water. " 'Tis so worn that I can see daylight through it. I fear the washing of it will make it disappear altogether."

"Be glad you do not have to sew the ladies' dresses — twelve stitches to the inch," said James. He squinted at the silken cloth in the dim light. "I will be blind by the time I grow me a beard. Alas, only Mr. Shakespeare gets all the candles he wants."

Kit squeezed the water out of the cloak. "Do you like it here?" he asked.

"Here?" James looked around the tiring house heaped with properties and costumes spilling out of crates. "To find anything is like looking for a flea on a sheepdog."

"No. Do you like the playhouse?"

" 'Tis not as good as our own that is locked up."

Kit shook his head. "I mean, do you like the life of a player?"

James put down his sewing. "I reckon I am as happy as a rat in a barn full of grain." He grinned at Kit. "When I was five, a company of players did come to my village. I could not understand much of the play, but I liked the tumblers and jigs. Most of all, I loved the clown who made me laugh. 'Tis what I want to be — a clown. Or as Mr. Shakespeare writes him — the fool."

"But Master Kemp is our clown."

"I know. That is why I must learn dancing and singing and rapiers and serious parts too. You must do it all, unless you are a most wondrous clown like Will Kemp."

Kit shook out the wet cloak and hung it over a rope stretched between the pillars. "Molly told me you lost a 'prentice a few months ago."

James nodded. "He did right well with the rapiers and had a most strong voice, but he could not learn lines to save his life. The bookkeeper had to read every cue to him from offstage."

"Do you think they would take me?" asked Kit.

"Take you where?"

"As a 'prentice player."

James studied Kit. "You know how hard we work now, but 'tis not the worst of it. In the summer they often close us down so the crowds will not spread the plague. We travel through the country then. In Puritan towns, they do not let us perform and run us out. In other places, if they have heard a rumor of plague, they move us on. And when we do give a play, sometimes we collect not even enough money to feed ourselves. I am always glad to come back to London in autumn."

Kit remembered Mr. Shakespeare's story of playing in Aldeburgh.

James went on. "You need to work hard, learn your lines, and speak them well. But more important is the fire inside you that keeps you here when Mr. Richard shouts at you for missing a line and spoiling his reply. Or the whole company is out of sorts, or Mr. Shakespeare writes lines we cannot speak to his liking. I may never be a great clown like Master Kemp, but the fire burns bright in me, and I must try."

Did Kit have such fire? He knew not, but said, "I want to try too."

James nodded and bent over his stitching again. "Speak you to Mr. Richard."

Kit frowned. "Could I not ask Mr. Cuthbert instead? He knows me right well." And likes me, Kit thought.

James shook his head. "Mr. Richard decides all matters of the players."

The next time Mr. Cuthbert sent for Kit to take a message to the Master of the Revels, Kit asked him anyway. "Sir, does not the company need another 'prentice player?"

Mr. Cuthbert looked blank. "A 'prentice?"

"You only have two now, and you did have three."

He stroked his chin. "Yes, truly."

Kit went on, before he lost his nerve. "I would like to be a player with the Chamberlain's Men."

Mr. Cuthbert smiled. "You want to stay on with us?"

"Yes, if it please you."

"It all depends on the accounts," he said, stroking his goose quill pen. "We will have the fee from the Queen, but all our expenses.... Perhaps in January." Then he frowned. "January...who knows of January...?" He rubbed his forehead and seemed to forget that Kit was there.

After a minute, Kit said, "Sir?"

Cuthbert started and looked up. "I have not the say of it. That comes from my brother. Now, off with you and that letter."

When Kit returned, Tom growled, "Where have you been?" Before Kit could answer, Tom said, "They need you on the stage."

Kit's heart skipped. Would he get a part in the play and appear before the Queen? He hurried to the freezing stage and found that the players had gone to the warm Hall of Revels. They needed Kit not to play a part, but to work on stage properties. Kit sighed and listened as Tom explained.

The Queen's hall was wide and tall. An artist would paint a huge forest scene on canvas, and the stage crew would take apart the frames of old scenery and reuse the lumber where they could. Then they had to build a throne, several benches, and the prow of a ship. Kit saw a new man come to help. It was Samuel, the chittering squirrel of a storyteller who worked for Peter Street.

Kit spent his days helping the stagehands measure, saw, nail, and sand. The sweet smell of sawdust carried him back to his grandsire's shop. He had made sawdust mountains and valleys when he was a small boy and had struggled to hold a hammer. Now the hammer fit his hand well enough. When he swung it, 'twas not so heavy, and he usually hit a nail on its head. As he worked, his grandsire's tunes came back to him, and he hummed as he sanded the seat of the bench.

Samuel sat next to Kit one day while they ate their pork pies in the tiring house, out of the sharp wind that blew across the stage. Samuel smacked his lips and ate as quickly as he talked. "Where did you learn the carpenter's trade? From you father?"

"My grandsire was a shipwright."

"Did he teach you? He must have taught you, yes he must," Samuel chattered.

"Teach me? No, sir. Though I did play about with his tools a goodly bit."

"Call me Samuel, not sir. No, sir, I am no sir." He laughed his chittering laugh. "But you, 'tis in your blood to be a carpenter," said Samuel, chewing hard.

Kit declared, "'Tis my fate to be a player, not a carpenter." Kit clamped his mouth shut. What if his words got back to Mr. Richard?

Samuel looked at Kit. "Are you not too old to begin?"

Kit could not change his story now. "I have already begun dancing lessons, and I will learn the rapier after the New Year. I played a few parts onstage already, with lines and all." What was he saying? He had said only a few "yes, my ladys." He looked around to see if anyone had heard him. No one was listening.

Samuel took a bite of pork pie and chewed. Then he wiped his mouth on his sleeve. "I would not take the life of a player, not if you gave it me on a golden platter. You have no guild to protect you. You are subject to the whims of your noble patrons. Ha!" He gave a sharp laugh. "Lords and noblemen! You cannot trust a man who does not work for his living."

Samuel chewed some more. "Then you are shut down by plagues. And the Puritans. They believe that plays are the work of the devil. The Puritans are getting stronger all the time; and if they have their way, they will close the playhouses forever. Then where would you be? Out on the street with no trade. No, give me the life of a carpenter. No one will ever outlaw the building of houses."

But no one claps and cheers for a carpenter, Kit thought.

Player

Kit saw James only at breakfast these days. He rehearsed until late at night and returned after Kit was asleep.

"They have got no end of wax candles at the Hall of Revels," James said. "Candles and coal fires and hot cider with cinnamon. I do not mind rehearsing till midnight."

One night James shook Kit, saying, "Wake you up!" Kit rolled over and blinked in the smoky light of a tallow candle.

James went on. "I cannot get my speech right. Sometimes Mr. Shakespeare's language is too clever by half. 'Tis smooth enough to listen to, but try speaking it!"

Kit yawned and sat up. The room was icy cold. He lay down again and pulled the blanket over his head. "Tell me in the morning," he mumbled.

James pulled off the blanket. "I need help now. You must be my bookkeeper. Mr. Richard said he will give the part to another boy if I do not have it right in the morning." He looked at Kit. "Can you read?"

Kit bristled. "Of course I can read. I went to school till I was ten. What must I do?"

James handed Kit a few sheets of paper. "You read Benedick's part, and I play Beatrice, a new part for me. Nicholas has played it till now. 'Tis from *Much Ado About Nothing*, and 'tis my first big part to play for the Queen."

James handed Kit a stump of a candle. Kit held it close to the pages filled with spidery writing. He had never seen a playbook before, for it was held close and locked away at the theatre. It was not the whole play, only one scene. "Where should I start?" he asked.

James showed him.

They went over and over the scene. James would remember one line, then forget the second line, or put the third line in its place. Finally, Kit noticed James could barely keep his head up. "Go to sleep," Kit said. "We will finish in the morning."

"Wake me early," James said, flopping into bed.

Next morning they worked until they heard the front door slam. "Everyone has left. I cannot be late," exclaimed James, grabbing his coat and rushing away.

"You do know it well," called Kit. As he stood up, James's

playbook fell to the floor. Kit picked it up and rushed to the window, but James was gone. Kit looked at the pages. Then he flung himself backward on the bed, kicking his legs in the air. "'Tis my chance!" he cried.

He would learn James's part. He had nearly memorized the lines already. With a little more practice, Kit could raise and lower his voice as James had done, to make Beatrice seem real. When he spoke it for Mr. Richard, he would become a player's apprentice, an official member of the Lord Chamberlain's Men. Fate was smiling on him at last.

"No, 'tis not how a girl picks up her skirt," said Molly. She picked up her own, to below the ankle, and stepped sideways. "Try you again."

Kit had learned his lines hours ago. He even remembered how James had spoken them. But James had not moved around the room when they practiced last night. Kit picked up his skirt to his knees, then dropped it to his ankles.

Molly sighed. "A good girl never shows that much leg."

"These are my feet," said Kit, looking down.

"But you lifted your skirt up to your knees first."

"Truly, skirts are right irksome," said Kit.

"They keep me warm in the winter and dry when it rains," said Molly. "'Tis better than rough trousers scratching all the time." She laughed.

"Do be serious!" cried Kit. He had not wanted to ask Molly for help. But James was at the Hall of Revels, and Kit wanted to play the scene perfectly. Molly and Kit rehearsed over and over.

"Is it possible disdain should die while she hath such meet food to feed it?"

Kit picked up his skirt and crossed in front of Molly, as if she were Benedick. "*Courtesy itself must convert to disdain, if you come in her presence.*" Then he turned his back and walked several steps away from her.

Finally Molly pronounced him nearly as good at Nicholas had been. But could he trust Molly? 'Twas Mr. Richard he had to please.

As Kit went to sleep that night, he murmured the lines to himself. The next morning, he spoke them aloud as he walked to the playhouse — "*Courtesy itself must convert . . .*" — ignoring the strange looks people gave him. He was ready.

For a week Kit waited. The few times Mr. Richard came to the playhouse, he hurried upstairs to see Mr. Cuthbert. So Kit kept on speaking his lines. "*. . . Disdain should die while she hath such meet food . . .*"

"What are you mumbling about?" asked Samuel one day as they painted the king's throne.

"Just a bit of nonsense," said Kit.

The next day, Samuel said, "The players will be here to rehearse with the properties tomorrow. Then we be on our way to Whitehall. Your first visit to the Queen's digs!" Samuel bobbed his head.

"'Tis most wonderful!" said Kit. He thought not of Whitehall, but of Mr. Richard. Tomorrow was his big day.

The next day the players arrived early. The performance was only a week away, and everyone was on edge, Richard Burbage most of all. He inspected the properties. "The throne is too high off the ground. Am I supposed to leap into it like a clown would do?"

He studied the painted scene. "That forest looks a bit weedy."

Kit approached Will Shakespeare who was examining the ship's prow.

"Sir..." said Kit.

Mr. Shakespeare turned and smiled. "Kit, how fare you?"

"Well enough, I trow. I build properties and such."

"So you are your grandsire's boy after all?"

Kit looked at his shoes. "I want to be a player, sir. I danced onstage a few weeks ago, and Mr. Phillips said I did well. I...I have been studying some lines to show Mr. Richard — and you, sir, if you will listen — so you will see that I am good enough." Kit raised his eyes. Mr. Shakespeare was smiling.

"So you took my advice."

"Sir?"

"You do lead your own dance."

Kit felt confused. Dance? Should he add a dance to his scene?

" 'Tis not the best time to see Richard. You would do well to wait."

"I pray you, sir!" begged Kit.

Will Shakespeare sighed. "I will do what I can."

In the afternoon, as Kit carried the properties outside to load the carts, Will Shakespeare came up to him.

"I think I can waylay Richard when he has finished with Cuthbert. Will you do this now, rather than after the Queen's play?"

"I do not want to wait," said Kit. "Shall I wear a costume?"

"As you wish. Come you to the stage and wait for us there."

Kit ran to the tiring house and found a petticoat. 'Twas not much, but he could show them what Molly had taught him. Raise the skirt to the ankles, no further. He spoke his lines as he dressed, then hurried to the stage. He saw Mr. Richard and Mr. Shakespeare coming down the stairs. His stomach lurched, but he took one deep breath, then another.

"So, you want to be a player, do you?" boomed Mr. Richard in his kingly voice.

"I do, sir," said Kit, looking him in the eye.

"We will hear you then."

Will Shakespeare and Richard Burbage sat on a bench at the corner of the stage. Kit stood close to them. "I will play Beatrice's part from Act One of *Much Ado About Nothing*," Kit said.

"Stand in the middle of the stage and play to the upper gallery," said Mr. Richard.

Kit walked to the middle and looked out into the playhouse. It was huge. With no groundlings to look at, he saw how tall the galleries were, how vast the space. He had never practiced his lines on the stage. He took a shaky breath and began. "*Is it possible —*"

"Speak up, boy. They will never hear you at the top," Mr. Richard said.

Kit looked up to the top galleries. His heart thrummed in his ears. His throat was dry as dust. He tried to swallow but could not. He took another shaky breath. "*Is it possible disdain should die . . . ?*"

What came next? He began again. "*Is it possible disdain should die . . . ?*"

Kit's memory went dark. His eyes darted to the two men who watched him. Mr. Richard frowned. Mr. Shakespeare smiled and gave him rest of the line. "*. . . while she hath such meet food to feed it . . . ?*"

"*Is it possible disdain should die when she hath such feet mood to foot it . . . ?*" Kit's voice shook. He knew he should lift his skirt and move to

73

the right, but his feet felt rooted to the stage while his heart thumped in his chest. He could not move or speak.

Mr. Shakespeare began, "*Courtesy itself* . . ."

"*Courtesy itself* . . ." But Kit could remember no more. The space seemed to grow larger, and he himself to grow smaller, until he felt like an ant waiting for a boot to crush him. The theatre began to spin, and Kit clutched his head.

"Stage fright," Mr. Shakespeare murmured. "*'As an imperfect player on the stage, who with his fear is put beside his part* . . .' "

"What say you, Will?" asked Mr. Richard.

" 'Tis a line from a sonnet I wrote."

Mr. Richard stood up. "The stage is not for everyone," he said to Kit.

Kit, still dizzy, walked over to him, tripping on his petticoat. "But I learned the lines, sir. I practiced the scene a hundred times. Perhaps if I practice it more. . . ."

Will Shakespeare said, "Learning your lines is one thing, performing them for two thousand people is quite another. You are not the only one who suffers from stage fright. I have seen players develop the affliction after ten years on the stage. Sometimes a particular role will bring it on, sometimes it comes from nowhere."

"Come, Will," said Mr. Richard. "We have no time to waste. 'Tis good of you to try, lad. You would never know what it was like, otherwise." He left the stage, but Mr. Shakespeare stayed behind.

"I am sorry." He laid a hand on Kit's shoulder.

"I know the scene, sir, I do," said Kit.

"There is other useful work in the playhouse."

"I want to do more than sweep floors!" cried Kit.

"Look at the ceiling. You could learn to do that."

Kit gazed up at the painting of a golden sun and figures of the zodiac. He looked at the peeling columns painted to look like marble. He looked at the prow of the ship. His grandsire had built a real ship that helped to save England from the Spanish Armada. Kit had helped to make one small prow of a mock ship that would not float in a mill pond.

"I want more than that," he said finally.

Mr. Shakespeare patted Kit's shoulder. "We will talk more after the Queen's performance," he said as he walked away.

Kit wrenched the petticoat over his head and heard it rip. He burst into tears and ran downstairs to the cellar under the stage. He collapsed into a corner and clutched the torn petticoat to his face to hide the sound of his howling sobs and catch the tears that ran down his face. The players called this place hell, for demons and ghosts rose up and dropped down from the trapdoor on the stage. The trapdoor was closed now, and the room was in darkness.

Kit had failed, frozen by fear that turned him to stone. Could he try again? Just the thought of that huge space beyond the stage made him feel ill. A light flashed into the basement. Kit stopped in midhowl.

Molly's face appeared upside down in the opening of the trapdoor. "Who is there?" she called.

Kit groaned. Molly was the last person he wanted to see.

"A stray dog, is it?" she asked.

Kit sat still, not even breathing.

"Blessed pudding, 'tis you! What are you rehearsing now, the part of a wolf?" She laughed. "Or perhaps —"

Kit leaped to his feet and stepped into the square of light. He shook his fist at Molly. "Stow you, you prating pest! Stow you! Why do you torment me all the time? Just pop off and...and...tidy your apple basket! I have had enough of your babble."

Molly's mouth dropped open and her upside-down face turned red.

"You...you..."

Kit heard no more. He ran up the stairs and out of the playhouse.

ACT THIRD

ACT THIRD, SCENE I

Secret Agent

When Kit awoke the next morning, he drifted from the comfort of sleep to the misery of the day before. He wanted to sleep again, to forget it all. But James was chattering on. "I do hope we please Her Majesty," he said.

Kit was going to take the stage properties to Whitehall today. On any other day he would be thrilled. Now he could just manage a weak smile. He had told James nothing of his trial with Mr. Richard, and so was spared his pity. That Mr. Shakespeare had seen him fail was shame enough.

Dark clouds hung low, mirroring Kit's gloom. As he loaded the properties onto the carts, his mood lifted, and his curiosity grew. If he could not play for the Queen, at least he would see her royal palace. But when he gathered the last armful of tools to take to Whitehall, Tom approached him and said, "Mr. Cuthbert wants you."

"Now? I am on my way to the palace," Kit said.

Tom scowled and walked away.

Kit frowned. "Samuel," he called, "I will meet you on the road. Mr. Cuthbert wants me."

Mr. Cuthbert smiled when Kit entered the room. "Ah, Kit, I need you today."

"But, sir, I was going to Whitehall."

"'Tis no matter. They can do the job without you."

Of course they can, thought Kit, and gloom descended upon him once more.

"I cannot do without you today." Mr. Cuthbert rested his elbows on the table and pressed his fingertips together to make a steeple. "As you know, we have tried to reach an accord with Giles Allen for months now. He refuses to renew our lease. He refuses to let us into our playhouse. He refuses even to discuss it anymore." Mr. Cuthbert pounded the table. "Now we hear rumors that he plans to tear down the Theatre and steal our timbers. The time for letters and lawyers is over. We are going to snatch our Theatre from Giles Allen, quick as a cutpurse." He thrust out his arm and snatched at the air.

Kit's face crumpled. He stared at his shoes.

Mr. Cuthbert peered at him. "What is wrong? Are you ill?"

Kit could not speak. He shook his head.

"Ah," Mr. Cuthbert said. "I did not mean to shame you, Kit. No one thinks of your . . . unfortunate incident anymore."

Kit did not stir.

Mr. Cuthbert leaned back in his chair. "You have redeemed yourself, my lad. I am pleased with your work, and others are too. You spoke about becoming a player's apprentice. I mean to talk to my brother about that. A handsome lad like you, you will soon be on the stage, bowing to thunderous applause." Mr. Cuthbert chuckled.

Kit's mouth went dry.

Mr. Cuthbert took a letter from his desk. "Take this to Peter Street as fast as you can fly." He peered over the desk at Kit's boots. "Have you still got Mercury's wings on your feet?" He laughed at his own wit.

Kit did not smile.

"After you deliver the letter, search the neighborhood and find every tradesman who owns a horse and cart. Ask them their fee for a day's work. We need the largest carts we can get."

"Why, sir? The properties are on their way to Whitehall," Kit said.

"Ah, yes, I did not finish my story. We are to rescue the Theatre from the clutches of Giles Allen," Mr. Cuthbert said dramatically. His right hand shot out once again.

Kit had seen players make such a gesture. Had Mr. Cuthbert tried to be a player when he was young? Perhaps Mr. Cuthbert had a fear of the stage, too. Or perhaps he was content to manage the business of the company and leave the applause to his brother.

"How will you rescue the Theatre?" asked Kit.

Mr. Cuthbert leaned forward and said in a low voice, " 'Twill be the most exciting drama ever to play on the streets of London." He paused.

Kit leaned toward him. Mr. Cuthbert did play the player.

"Peter Street and his crew of carpenters will take apart the playhouse, joist by joist, beam by beam. Then we will take it across the river to Southwark and build the finest playhouse England has ever seen. With those timbers in hand, we can just afford to do it. All Giles Allen will get is a pile of worthless rubble." Mr. Cuthbert sat back and grinned.

A jumble of pictures floated through Kit's mind, of the old playhouse tumbling down and rising up again.

Mr. Cuthbert interrupted Kit's visions. "'Twill not be easy. 'Twill be downright dangerous. And you, my lad, will play a part in this drama. You are my secret agent. Be off with this letter. We have not a minute to waste." He held out the letter, then drew it back. "Tell no one of this, not the carters, not even the others in the company. Cloak and dagger and all that, just like on the stage."

"You can trust me, sir," said Kit.

"I know I can," Mr. Cuthbert said, handing over the letter.

Kit jogged down Bishopsgate, humming as he went. He saw a patch of blue up in the cloudy London sky. What a turn the day had taken. Stealing the playhouse right out from under Mr. Allen's nose. Could they do it? At London Bridge, Kit saw Samuel and the others loading the properties onto river barges. He glanced at the letter in his hand. It could wait a few minutes. He tucked it inside his shirt and scrambled down the riverbank.

Samuel jumped out of the barge and said, "You are here in good time, though you did manage to shun the work. We are ready to go, ready to go." He made a low bow and swept his arm before him. "Her Majesty awaits you, Sir Kit."

Kit replied, "I cannot go. I have to run errands for Mr. Cuthbert today."

"Bad luck," said Samuel, clucking his tongue. "I'll give the Queen your regrets."

"You do that," said Kit with a grin. He felt a pang, but oddly 'twas not a great one. He was thrilled with the promise of a dangerous drama — and glad that Mr. Cuthbert trusted him with the secret. Kit walked along the river toward Peter Street's warehouse, watching the barges until they slipped out of sight.

Master Street nodded, then shook his head as he read Cuthbert Burbage's letter. When he finished, he sighed and drummed his fingers on the table. They drummed faster and faster until Master Street noticed them and stopped. "It helps me think out a problem," he said.

"Have you an answer, sir?" asked Kit.

"I will write it out and send it to him later." He began drumming his fingers again.

Kit spoke up. "Mr. Cuthbert told me your plan, and I have a question. Will not Mr. Allen discover our scheme? Will he not call the sheriff to arrest us?"

"Allen is at his country house for the Christmas season. 'Tis what we have been waiting for. We are counting on the favor of Dame Fortune — and the neighbors — to prevent him from learning what we do."

"How long will it take?"

"I do not know, Kit. I have never done such work before. It will take" — he drummed his fingers on the table again — "about four months to build the new playhouse. Perhaps a few days to take apart the old one."

Kit spent the rest of the day searching out men with carts to hire.

"When do you need me?" asked one carter.

"I do not know," answered Kit. "Perhaps in a week."

"I might be dead in a week. Come you then and ask again."

"How many days' work?" asked another.

"I do not know," said Kit.

"Well, neither do I. When you tell me, I'll tell you my price."

"What will I carry? Something illegal?" asked still another.

"I cannot say, sir," replied Kit.

"It does not mean I will not do the job. I would charge more though. Who is your master?"

Kit thought for a moment. "I cannot tell you that either," he said finally.

Handing his list of carters' names to Mr. Cuthbert, Kit said, "The carters want to know more than I can tell them."

Mr. Cuthbert looked at the list. "We will find them when we need them." He began to scribble on a piece of paper. "On December 26 we perform *Henry IV, Part II*, and January 1 we do *Much Ado About Nothing*. December 27 we bring the properties from *Henry* back here.

"December 31, we transport the properties for *Much Ado*. That gives us three days, December 28, 29, and 30. Giles Allen will likely return to London after the New Year. Hmm." Mr. Cuthbert studied the dates. He looked at Kit. "Three days. What do you think, Kit?"

"We will do it, sir!" he exclaimed. His voice sounded sure, but what did he know of such business? He had been sure of his future as a player, and he had been dead wrong.

ACT THIRD, SCENE II

Thribbler

Kit arrived at the Theatre early on December 28. For the last few days, as everyone feasted on Christmas goose and mince pies, he had heard about nothing but the players' grand triumph before the Queen. Another drama awaited today, though, and he would play a part in this one.

He had not slept much in the night and crept out of the house before anyone was awake. It was still dark, but falling snow gave the scene a ghostly glow. Standing in the doorway of the playhouse, out of the storm, he stamped his feet and slapped his arms across his chest to keep warm. After a while, he heard muffled footsteps and saw lanterns bobbing through a veil of whiteness. Was it the sheriff and his constables?

"All right, men, circle the building and stand guard," called Richard Burbage. A dozen players, including Nicholas and James, came into sight. Kit was startled to see them carrying rapiers, axes, and halberds. Mr. Cuthbert had said it might be dangerous. Kit thought he had meant tearing down the building.

Peter Street, the master carpenter, and his men came up behind the players, carrying bundles of tools.

"Hello, Kit," called Samuel, shaking his head to scatter the snow that had dusted it. His light brown hair glowed in the lantern light.

Master Street addressed the carpenters. "We must first make an entrance. We could break down the door, but I want to save those timbers. Our best solution is to make an opening between the beams and remove bricks enough to crawl through."

He looked at Kit. "If we were all as lean as Kit, we would have quick work of it. But because Edward is here"—he glanced at a stout man standing next to Kit—"we will make the entry a fair size bigger."

Everyone laughed. Even Edward. Even Kit.

Peter Street wielded a sledgehammer, smashing the plaster that covered the bricks of the outer wall. When they had broken through and entered the playhouse, they climbed to the top gallery. Peter Street explained that they would work on one level at a time, breaking the plaster walls and the wooden lath until only the oak beams stood. Then they would move down to the second gallery and do the same, and finally to the lowest level of seats. "Tie a cloth round your face to save you breathing too much plaster," said Master Street.

Kit went to work. He found that he had not the strength to break the plaster. He looked at Samuel's arms and thought of his grandsire. It would take years to build such muscles. He tried to rip out the woven strips of wood that formed the lath, but that took a man's strength as well.

So Kit carried away small chunks of plaster and tossed them over the edge of the gallery. *Thud!* They fell on the ground far below, the ground that he had cleaned and raked so often.

When the chunks of plaster proved too heavy to lift, he stomped on them to break them into smaller pieces. He gathered armloads of lath and tossed them to the ground. The wood strips did not fall so heavily. Kit could make them twirl through the air as they fell.

The day was bitterly cold, but the work kept him warm. The sun must have risen, but they would not see it that day. A dull light revealed a near solid wall of white, as snow kept falling. Kit could not see across the playhouse to where the other men worked. He could only hear the pounding of their hammers, and even this was muffled by the falling snow. 'Twas a strange ghostly world.

Molly called from the ground, "I have got food here! Meat pies and ale for all!"

Kit had not spoken to her since that day he wanted to forget, and he did not want to see her now.

"Come get something to eat from the lass," Samuel said, putting down his crowbar.

"I be not hungry," Kit declared.

Samuel rubbed his hand together, reminding Kit again of a nervous squirrel. "Suit yourself, suit yourself." But when he returned he handed Kit a meat pie. "Here is some fuel to fire your belly. I do not want you slowing down on the job."

Kit mumbled his thanks. He truly was hungry.

Master Street came to inspect the work. "You make good progress," he said.

"Kit is a boon, he is," said Samuel. "I do not have to stop and chuck the rubbish over the gallery. He chucks it for me."

Master Street nodded. "Keep working. We will not have daylight past four o'clock, and the sheriff could arrive at any time."

Not long after, Kit heard shouting outside.

"I thought there might be trouble," said Samuel. "Is it Allen, or the neighbors, or the sheriff?" He tugged Kit's arm. "Come you, come. Your players may need our help. They have weapons, but so do we." He picked up a hammer, Kit grabbed a chisel, and they hurried down the stairs.

Outside a crowd had gathered. Mr. Richard stood in front of a few players holding rapiers. They were covered in snow, frozen like snowmen. Nicholas and James held their halberds high. The long poles towered above the crowd, and the curved blades pointed forward. Mr. Shakespeare stood with them, but held no weapon.

"Once again, I order you to cease and desist," called a man in the crowd.

"Who are you to order me?" demanded Mr. Richard.

"I am Henry Johnson, a friend of Giles Allen," said a fat man in a long coat. "I hold his power of attorney."

"'Tis of no interest to me," said Mr. Richard.

"You are trespassing on his property!"

"My brother and I own this building." He nodded to the players, who moved closer to Henry Johnson, rapiers drawn.

"Common thieves, all of you," shouted Johnson, his face turning red with anger. "You, Peter Street, are you directing this work?"

"I am," he said, stepping forward.

Johnson shook his fist. "You will all go to prison for stealing Giles Allen's property," he shouted.

"Stealing? No, sir," Peter Street replied calmly. "We are taking the timbers apart to build them in another form. Giles Allen means to build a new building on this site."

Kit looked at Master Street. He was playing a part.

"You speak falsely," said Henry Johnson. "I know of the legal battles these *players*" — he spat out the word with disgust — "have been waging against Allen. You mean to steal these timbers from him." He turned to the crowd and shouted, "Will no one act with me against these common thieves?"

No one answered. The people lived nearby and had seen the players coming and going for years. They took no sides in this dispute. However they were most curious about this drama being played out-of-doors.

Henry Johnson turned to Peter Street and demanded, "If you do work for Giles Allen, then why are the players brandishing weapons?"

Richard Burbage gave Henry Johnson his sternest look. "As it happens, we come from a rehearsal," he said. "We play for Her Majesty Queen Elizabeth in three days."

Kit felt the tension between the two men stretch as tight as a tuned

89

lute string. Without thinking he shouted, "Happy Christmas, Mr. Johnson! Happy Christmas, neighbors!"

A few nervous laughs broke out. Then Mr. Richard plunged into the crowd, shaking hands and patting boys' heads. The players sheathed their rapiers and strolled among the crowd, wishing people good tidings of the season. Boys swarmed to see the weapons.

Will Shakespeare clapped Kit on the back. "That was a skillful thribble you tossed out, my lad." Then he melted back into the crowd.

Samuel cocked his head. "A thribble?"

Kit replied, "Thribbling is the talk players make up to answer the hecklers in the audience."

"So, you are a thribbler, soon to take your place onstage with your master thribblers?"

"I have no master," Kit muttered.

Samuel drew back with a look of mock horror. "No master? You could be picked up by the constable as a rogue and a vagabond!"

Kit turned away. He could not jest about his situation. Someone began to sing; and Will Shakespeare took the hand of a woman and twirled her around, as he had done with Kit that day on the stairway. Soon the whole crowd was singing and dancing. Mr. Johnson stormed away down the road.

"Good tidings to you, Mr. Johnson," Richard Burbage called.

Mr. Johnson turned and sputtered, "You have not seen the last of me. I will bring the sheriff next time."

"Come, men, back to work," said Peter Street.

"'Twas quite a tale you told them, sir," said Kit, "about doing Mr. Allen's bidding."

"'Twas not exactly a lie, just a bit of thribbling. These timbers *will* be used for a new playhouse; and when Giles Allen finds his land vacant, doubtless he *will* build a new building." Peter Street grinned. "Where are the other apprentices? We need them to do the work that you are doing. I think the danger of an armed attack has passed for today."

Kit pointed out Nicholas and James, still holding their halberds. Master Street spoke to Mr. Richard, and the two boys followed Peter Street into the Theatre. "Kit will tell you what to do," he said.

Kit explained how he cleared away the plaster and lath. He rather enjoyed giving orders to Nicholas, who scowled at him.

"I am not a common laborer," muttered Nicholas.

Kit said nothing.

"We will be warmer doing such work," said James. "I am near frozen just standing all day while the snow covered us."

By afternoon they had taken away the walls of the upper gallery and moved downstairs.

"We will not finish in three days at this rate," said Master Street. "We have only two hours of daylight left. Henry Johnson called us common thieves. We must live up to the name and finish this job quickly!"

Kit grinned. When he threw down the next load of twirling lath, he twirled in a circle himself and clapped his hands over his head. 'Twas a dance of a merry thribbler.

Puny Urchin

The following day the sun shone, and the snow-covered rubble glittered like a mound of diamonds. Nicholas continued to grumble about working with the carpenters. "I am a player, not a scavenger."

James worked as best he could, but he had a coughing fit every few minutes. "My lungs be not strong," he said.

Kit tried to help James as well as Samuel. He carried rubble all morning, ignoring his aching arms. When the plaster and lath had been removed, the giant oak timbers shone silvery gray against the brilliant blue winter sky. Then Samuel began to loosen the wooden pegs that held the beams together. Kit found a chisel and did the same.

"Unless we have a terrible tempest, the building will stand with loose joints for one night," Samuel said as he worked. "Tomorrow we will remove the pegs and pull down the beams."

Peter Street moved from bay to bay in the playhouse. He cut notches in the timbers.

"What are you doing, sir?" asked Kit.

"These timbers have warped over the last twenty years," Master Street said. He pointed to a crossbeam. "This beam will fit only into this one," he said, pointing to a vertical post, "and not into any other. When we build the new playhouse, we must needs match them up again. The new playhouse will go together exactly as the old one does."

"What do those slashes mean?" asked Kit. "My grandsire used them too."

"Your grandsire?" asked Master Street.

"He was a shipbuilder."

"Ah, that explains it."

"Sir?"

"Your way with tools. But not just that. You want to know how and why we do things, and even better, you think of the whole job. Samuel did not tell you to clear the space. You saw what needed doing, and did it."

Kit blushed. He felt more awkward with praise than he did with scorn.

"How old are you, Kit?"

"Twelve, sir."

"A bit young." Master Street looked around the Theatre. "But 'tis no time to talk. We have to finish here today, and carry away the timber tomorrow."

"And the notches, sir?"

"Oh, yes." He rubbed a callused finger along a notch in the beam. "Those are the markings for the men who do not read. Can you read, Kit?"

"Yes, sir, and I can write too."

Peter Street nodded. "Would you help me mark?"

"Yes, sir." They walked around the Theatre, stopping at each bay to make notches in the timbers. The building was fast becoming a skeleton. Many questions came to Kit about timbers and buildings, but he did not bother Master Street with them now.

Mr. Cuthbert arrived in midafternoon. He stumbled through the rubble, then up the stairs. "Is everything on schedule?" he asked.

"Yes," answered Peter Street. "We will load the carts in the morning. All will be safe in my warehouse by tomorrow nightfall. You ordered the carts to be here before dawn."

Mr. Cuthbert pursed his lips. "Surely you did that."

Peter Street looked stricken. "'Tis not what we agreed."

The two men stared at each other.

Finally Peter spoke. "You mean we have not got the carts hired?"

Kit watched the two men. Cuthbert's jaw dropped, and he stood speechless.

Peter Street drummed his fingers on the railing. "I sent a message to you a week ago."

"It did not arrive."

"'Twas that lazy apprentice of mine. He shall be sorry for this."

His fingers drummed faster. "You must choose, Cuthbert. You have two carts hired for the Queen's performance. We can use those carts and make many trips over several days. But then you cannot take the properties to the palace for the New Year's play. Or you can take the properties and leave the timbers here until after the New Year. But Giles Allen will likely be back in town then."

Cuthbert looked as pale as the snow that covered the ground. "These timbers are our future. Without them we cannot build a playhouse, and without a playhouse the company will fail. But to fail the Queen . . . we cannot do that either!"

Tense silence enveloped the two men. The sounds of hammering and crashing plaster echoed around the building.

"Mr. Cuthbert?" Kit dared to speak. "I will go to the carters I found last week and try to hire them for tomorrow."

The two men looked at Kit. Cuthbert said, "I still have the list you gave me."

"You will probably pay double at such short notice," Peter Street said.

Mr. Cuthbert winced. "Thus vanishes our profit from the Queen."

"The choice is yours," said Peter Street.

Mr. Cuthbert sighed. "Very well, we must do the job tomorrow. I will fetch Kit's list."

"I will calculate again the number of carts," said Peter Street.

Kit looked up at the Theatre. The silvery beams seemed to glow against the darkening indigo sky. The last act of this drama was about to begin. Would he find enough carters? Would they remove the timbers in time? Mr. Johnson might return with the sheriff. Mr. Allen might return to London tonight, and all would be lost.

Or perhaps the drama would end as a comedy. Master Street and his men would take the timbers down, move them through the city, and lock them away until spring. Then —

"Kit!" Mr. Cuthbert came huffing and puffing, stumbling over the pile of plaster. He had the list in his hand. "You and Samuel search for the carters. You can show him where they live, and he can strike the best bargain. And may Dame Fortune smile on you, or we are lost!"

Kit and Samuel trudged through the streets as the winter sun set. Some shops were closed, as people celebrated the twelve days of Christmas. Other carters, seeing how eager the two were, charged three times their usual price. Samuel, nattering and chattering, could sometimes bargain them down to twice their fee. It was long after dark when they had finished their work, but they had hired six carts.

"I must needs be off to meet my mates at the tavern," said Samuel. "Will you take the news to Master Street?"

"I will," said Kit.

"There's a good lad," said Samuel, clapping Kit on the back before he strolled away.

Kit walked toward the river. He passed a tavern bursting with people talking and laughing.

> "Jolly good luck to the pint pot,
> Good luck to the Barley Mow,
> Here's the pint pot, half a pint, gill pot, half a gill, quarter gill,
>   nipperkin, and the brown bowl."

Kit sighed. Would he ever have friends to meet in the tavern? James was friendly now, but when he became a famous player, would he bother with Kit? Alone on the streets without a master, Kit could get picked up and sent to the orphanage at Christ's Hospital, or worse, the workhouse at Bridewell. There he would walk a treadmill all day to grind the grain to pay for his keep.

A group of rowdy boys passed him. They were dressed in blue, the uniform of all apprentices. These were boys with masters. They had work now and a future protected by the guild of their trade. Apprentices rose to be masters, and masters could become wealthy. Everyone knew the story of Dick Whittington, the poor apprentice who became Lord Mayor of London. One of the lads shoved Kit and nearly knocked him down. Kit raised his arms to shove him back. The boy was not the Lord Mayor yet, just a rowdy boy on the street. But the boy smiled and said, "Beg pardon, mate," and hurried on.

Kit turned down a lane to take a shortcut to Master Street's house. The only light came from behind the shutters in the houses. Kit slipped on the icy ruts and nearly fell. Around a bend he saw three lads coming toward him, laughing loudly. He heard one voice above the rest.

"And then said I, 'If you bullyrag me, you will not be prowling the streets no more. You will sit in the mud with your two legs broke, begging for farthings.' "

Kit knew that voice. He looked for an alley to duck into, but saw none. He looked over his shoulder. If he tried to run, the three would catch him. His only hope was to slink past them. He ducked his head and moved to the edge of the lane.

Roger's barking laugh filled the air. "'Tis our old friend Kit

Bungles, who could not cut a purse from a fence post without knocking the fence post down!" The two boys, Ginger and Big Ears, laughed too. "'Tis not wise to be all alone in a dark lane, Master Bungles. There be rough rogues about who could do you harm."

Kit tried to walk around him, but Roger blocked his escape. "Why do you hurry? 'Tis not courteous to ignore those what is right courteous to you."

"I have business," said Kit. "Let me pass." He looked straight at Roger and declared, "I stayed away from you. Now stay away from me."

"Will you listen to him," cried Roger as he pushed Kit against the wall. "He is too good for us, now that he is hobbing and nobbing with coves what wear fine clothes and play upon the stage. Do not look so shocked. I've got spies what keep an eye on you."

"Let me go." Kit lurched forward to find a way past Roger, but Ginger and Big Ears moved in closer.

Roger turned to the boys. "What say we strike a peg into his lordship?"

"Aye, Roger," they said. They grabbed Kit's arms, but he pulled one arm free. His hand shot sideways and hit Ginger in the face. Blood gushed from Ginger's split lip.

Roger raised his fist and snarled, "No one thrashes my mates."

Kit held up his hands. "I meant no harm. See, I will help him." He leaned forward to wipe the blood from Ginger's chin.

Roger grabbed Kit's arm and flung him to the ground. Kit cried out, and Roger jeered, "Look at the mangy dog, yelping and bothering the neighbors." He gave Kit a kick in the ribs. Big Ears joined in kicking as Kit tried to roll away from them. But all three surrounded him.

"Stop, I pray you!" he shouted.

Roger gave a loud laugh.

"I pray you, Roger," Kit cried again.

Big Ears mocked him in a whining voice. "I pray you, Roger!"

"Clubs, clubs!" came a shout from the end of the lane. "Clubs, clubs!"

"A brawl!" yelled Roger. "'Tis the 'prentices looking to fight!" He stepped away from Kit. "I would rather brawl with lusty coves. Where is the fun in beating a puny urchin?" Roger gave Kit a final kick that knocked the breath out of him. Then he and his boys ran down the lane.

Kit lay on the ground, struggling for breath as the shouting grew fainter. Finally he stood up. His ribs hurt and his left ankle felt tender, but no bones seemed broken. He limped down the lane, looking both ways before he turned right.

He had been lucky this time. But what about tomorrow and the day after that? He couldn't roam the streets safely without a mate or two — or a whole pack. He needed a master and a place for himself where he could find such mates. A gust of wind blew icy sleet into his face as he limped toward the river. He ducked his head to avoid the blast.

Nimble-Toes

Next morning the gray light of the coming dawn revealed the bare beams of the Theatre. Master Street seemed to be everywhere at once, pointing out what to do and where to go. Kit worked alongside Samuel, prying the loose pegs out of the beams one by one, and throwing them into a sack. Last night's beating seemed a world away, but Samuel noticed his limp.

I slipped on the cobbles," said Kit. "'Tis nothing. Should we mark the pegs with numbers?"

"No need, no need," said Samuel. "Many are cracked and broken, you see. We cannot use those again." He held up an unbroken peg. "But waste not, want not," he said as he tossed the peg into a sack.

Two brawny men worked beside Samuel and Kit, prying the crossbeams loose from the upright beams. When all the pegs were removed, Kit went outdoors to find a jumble of horses, carts, workmen, timbers, and curious neighbors. The workmen shouted, the neighbors gossiped, and one or two horses neighed.

"Clear the way, clear the way!" Samuel called as he nudged people back to allow workers to load the beams on the carts. The carts were too short for some timbers. Men had to walk behind them, balancing the ends of the beams on their shoulders to keep them from falling off.

Back and forth they went from the Theatre to Peter Street's warehouse. Kit helped to load the carts, then stacked the next load as he waited for the carts to return. At midday Samuel said, "Kit, you climb on to keep this load steady. 'Tis a heavy one."

After Kit had settled himself on top of the beams, Samuel climbed up and laid a coil of rope on Kit's head. " 'Tis a royal procession with the queen, and nobles holding up her chair." Everyone laughed.

"Long live the Queen!" shouted Samuel.

Kit frowned.

"Come now, Kit, 'tis good fun," said Samuel.

Kit saw they were not mocking him, so he grinned and gave a royal wave as the horses set off.

When they reached the city gate, Samuel, who balanced a heavy beam on his shoulder, said, "This is the risky part. We be only a few blocks away from the sheriff's office."

Kit kept a sharp eye out for any armed men coming their way, but he saw only ordinary people going about their daily business. The players' luck was holding.

The markets were less crowded than usual, this being Christmas week. But London streets were never empty of boys. They hooted and hollered as the cart made its way down Bishopsgate. Their elders stared at the strange procession of horses, carts, a building taken apart and Kit on top of it all. Two boys tried to climb on the wagon, but their mothers held them back.

"What have you there?" called a man.

"A pack of bones," replied Kit.

"Where is it going?"

"To the river," he shouted. Peter Street's warehouse was close to the Thames.

"In the river? Over the bridge?"

"Yes!" shouted Kit, and the crowd laughed.

None of the crowd followed them that far, but a player, with rapier at hand, stood at the door of the warehouse. Kit helped the carter hold the horses as the men unloaded the beams.

"Quickly," called Samuel. "We have more trips to make."

When they returned to the playhouse, the tallest timbers were coming down. All the workmen and many of the players clutched ropes tied to a beam. Peter Street shouted orders to each team to move or remain still, tighten or loosen the rope. Kit stood near Mr. Shakespeare, well back from the work. "My future lies in the strength and steadiness of those men," Mr. Shakespeare said.

As they watched, the beam tilted toward the ground.

"Keep it steady!" Peter Street shouted to the men. One team strained to let out their rope slowly. Kit saw their faces turn red. Another team pulled up the slack on the rope to ensure a smooth descent.

"Stop!" yelled a voice behind them. Henry Johnson, Giles Allen's man, stood with his arms in the air.

Peter Street turned to look, then turned back to his men. "Do not stop!" he called. "Steady on. Down, down." The beam dropped slowly until it rested on the ground.

Henry Johnson said, "Still trespassing, I see! Giles Allen will be back in London tonight, and he will set the sheriff on you." He shook his fist and sputtered, "You will not get away with this."

Peter Street replied, "Get away or get killed!"

Mr. Johnson looked up to see another beam tilting his way. He backed up, tripped, fell down, and then scurried away on hands and knees.

Kit laughed.

Henry Johnson stood up, brushing snow from his coat, and frowned at Kit. "What is your part in all this?" he demanded.

Kit shrugged. "I am but a ninnyhammer."

"A ninnyhammer for certain!" Mr. Johnson tossed his head and marched away, leaving his dignity behind him in the snow.

The sun was close to setting as the final beam was lowered to the ground. The carters had tied three carts together to hold the longest beams, with three teams of horses hitched together in front.

Master Street said, "Players, go you and persuade the gatekeepers to keep the city gate open until we get there." Kit followed Will Kemp, the clown.

At the city wall, a big-bellied gatekeeper said, "Gates close at dusk. You know that."

"The sun's just set, we've got time yet," chanted Will Kemp. "Throw me a glance, and I'll give you a dance!" He flung off his cloak to reveal five pairs of bells on his legs.

When he stomped the ground he set himself a-jingling. Then he began to dance as one man played a pipe and drummed the tabor:

"He married his wife in the month of June,
Risselty-rossilty, now now now.
He carried her off in a silver spoon.
Risselty-rossilty, hey bom-bossety,
Nicholasety-nackety, retrical quality,
Willaby-wallaby, now now now."

People hurrying to enter and leave the city stopped to listen. Big Belly jostled the crowd. "Bawl all you like, the gates are closing. Move along now."

The crowd ignored him and began clapping to Will Kemp's steps.

Kit kept watch for the last carts. Finally he saw them. The horses were not used to working in a team of six, and it took four men to guide them. Closer and closer the carts lumbered, as darker and darker the sky grew. The gatekeeper began to unlatch the heavy gates. Kit ran to the carts, grabbed two wooden stakes, and ran back to the gate. He hopped up and down in front of Big Belly, clacking his sticks and singing:

"Jog on, jog on the footpath way and merrily hent the stile-a,
Your merry heart goes all the day. Your sad one tires in a mile-a."

A hint of a smile lit old Big Belly's face as Kit kept up his clamor until the strange procession reached the gate. When the last cart had clattered through, Big Belly closed the city gates with a thud and drew the latch.

Now Will Kemp danced down the road, and a plump woman leaped alongside him. Nicholas and James joined in but, having no bells, they jingled not like Will Kemp.

"Risselty-rossilty, hey bom-bossety,
Nicholasety-nackety, retrical quality,
Willaby-wallaby, now now now."

"Join the dance," said Will Shakespeare in his ear.

"Shall I?" Kit asked.

Mr. Shakespeare winked.

Kit slipped into the middle of the dancers. There was Molly, leaping and skipping. Molly! He stumbled and lost the beat. Then he danced ahead of her and caught up with Will Kemp.

"Your new name be Nimble-Toes," said Kemp as he circled round Kit.

Kit grinned and leaped high. The torchlight, the music, the dancing, and the rumble of the carts filled him with gladness. The day's drama had turned into a comedy after all, and he had played his own part well.

ACT FOURTH

ACT FOURTH, SCENE I

Apprentice

January brought snow, rain, and gray skies. Whenever Kit saw Molly, she was rubbing her crippled hand. Not many people braved the bitter weather to attend plays, but the company pressed on. Kit returned to scattering nutshells on the ground and scrubbing mud from the stage. He had lost track of the number of weeks he had worked at the playhouse, but surely his punishment was nearing an end. What would happen to him then?

Yet as the days and weeks passed, Kit realized that he had grown attached to life at the playhouse. He liked the plays he saw or, rather, heard from the tiring house. He liked the drama off the stage too — the spats between players and the feud with Giles Allen. But most of all, he liked the sense of belonging. So one day Kit climbed two flights of stairs and made his way past heaps of costumes to Mr. Cuthbert's desk in the corner of the attic.

"I come to ask, sir, if you could find a place for me in the company," Kit said.

Mr. Cuthbert clapped his hands. "Ah, yes, you want to be a player."

"Not a player."

Mr. Cuthbert's eyebrows shot up. "Not a player?"

"No, sir." Kit stared at the king's cloak draped over the rafters above Mr. Cuthbert's head.

"I seem to remember 'twas your heart's desire."

"I cannot do it," Kit said, shifting from one foot to another. "I tried to speak some lines to Mr. Richard and Mr. Shakespeare, and I froze with fright."

"I see," said Mr. Cuthbert. He leaned forward. "Well, I hear you are a nimble dancer. Perhaps you could dance and join the crowd scenes as a hired man."

Kit shook his head. "I want a steady place in the company, not the rootless life of a hired man."

Mr. Cuthbert looked at Kit a long moment, then said, "Would the work behind the stage suit you? Building properties and grinding the winch for the flying spirits? You proved to be a useful hand when we prepared the Queen's play."

"Will that give me a place in the company?"

"We could take you on as an apprentice stage boy. We do not

have an official guild, you know, but we would bind you with a contract. Apprentices usually pay a premium, but perhaps we could forgo that."

Kit was confused by all the details. "Then I will have a steady place with the Chamberlain's Men?"

"You will not be paid for seven years, but you will learn all that Tom can teach you, and you will go on living with Mr. Phillips."

"And I will have a steady place?"

Mr. Cuthbert smiled. "Yes, you will have a steady place. If you agree, I will arrange it with the others." Then his smile faded, and he looked hard at Kit. "Are you sure this is what you want?"

"Yes, sir, 'tis what I want."

"Will Shakespeare tells us he is writing some new plays. Let us hope they will bring in bigger audiences, so we can all keep our places in the company."

Next morning as Kit cleaned the ground, he thought of the time he had thrown down his sack and run away, angry at everyone. He recalled dancing with his broom, filled with the hope of being a player. Now he was not dancing, but he was not running away either.

Giles Allen had come back to London to find a pile of broken plaster where the Theatre had been. He filed one lawsuit against Richard and Cuthbert Burbage, and another against Peter Street. They, in turn, filed lawsuits against Giles Allen.

"Just listen to this," Mr. Cuthbert said to Kit one day. "'Tis the suit of Giles Allen against us." He held a closely-written paper close to the candle.

"*The said Cuthbert Burbage unlawfully combining and confederating himself with the said Richard Burbage and one Peter Street, with diverse other persons to the number of twelve . . .*" Mr. Cuthbert looked up and chuckled. "How does he know how many we were? I do not even know."

He went on reading, "*. . . did riotously assemble themselves together and armed with diverse and offensive weapons, namely swords, daggers, bills, axes, and such . . .*" Mr. Cuthbert looked up again. "He did forget our halberds. Wait, there is more." He read again, "*. . . in very riotous and outrageous and forcible manner attempted to pull down the said Theatre and did in the most forcible and riotous manner take and carry away all the wood and timber thereof.*"

He said to Kit, "What say you to that?"

"The only 'forcible manner' I remember is that of the building holding fast against us as we pulled apart those beams. But he did leave out our 'riotous' dancing through the streets." Kit grinned.

"'Twould be right comical if 'twere not so vexatious and expensive," said Mr. Cuthbert. "He *knows* that timber belongs to us. Yet still he tries to take it from us."

Nearly every day, Kit delivered messages back and forth to the courthouse, the playhouse, or Peter Street's warehouse. Kit often lingered at the warehouse. 'Twas not any warmer inside than outside, but he liked to breathe in the smell of wood and sawdust.

Peter Street shaved an oak plank with a chisel. "A thousand people move to London every month," he told Kit. "Most of them are young boys, come to make their fortune. But even boys need a bed to sleep in, a room for the bed, and a house filled with such rooms. We build the house frames here, then take them apart like we did at the Theatre. When the weather is fine, we put them together again on the building site. London is growing far beyond its walls, and I do not believe 'twill stop anytime soon," he said. "I will never be short of work."

Kit knew that those boys moving to London fancied a bit of fun too. As long as they could find it at a playhouse, there would be work for a stage-keeper. He had signed his apprenticeship papers and had a secure place for himself at last. 'Twas not such a bad fate. He could think of worse.

In February Kit heard a noisy quarrel between Will Kemp and Will Shakespeare.

"I am the player they come to watch," cried Will Kemp, pacing back and forth across the stage. "Without me, you will not draw enough of a crowd to feed even this 'prentice his bit of bread and beer." He pointed to Kit, who was collecting the trash from yesterday's play.

Will Shakespeare shouted, "I will not have jigs in my new plays. Such bawdy skits and coarse language — no!"

"Then I will take them elsewhere," roared Kemp, "and you will rue this day!"

"My new plays are different," insisted Shakespeare. "They will have wit enough for everyone, even you, Will Kemp, and a dance now and then. But no...more...jigs!" Kit heard his passion echo off the top gallery. "...no...jigs."

"You mewling poet!" Will Kemp nearly spat the words at Will Shakespeare. "See if you even have a company after I am gone. 'Tis my jigging people love best."

With that Will Kemp walked out on the Chamberlain's Men.

"Mr. Kemp means to dance all the way to Norwich, ninety miles away," James told Kit a few days later.

"Is it possible?" exclaimed Kit.

James shrugged. "He asked me to go with him. He means to attract great crowds on the road, and gold pieces too. After Norwich he means to go to Europe and dance in Rome, in Venice, in Jerusalem! Why he even talks of dancing over the Alps!"

"Will you go?" asked Kit.

James sighed. "I grieve to see him go. He is the best master I could have, but 'tis best for me to stay with the company."

On February 26, James and Kit rose as the church bells rang six o'clock. They stole out of the house and made their way to Guildhall, the ancient building where the Lord Mayor and his aldermen met. A crowd had gathered outside, and in the middle stood Will Kemp.

His servant tried to tie bells on Will's legs, but he made the job difficult by striding up and down, jesting with the audience. As Kit and James drew close, he called out, "And here, good people, are two young dancers from the Chamberlain's Men. Come you and show what you can do!"

Kit hesitated, but James pushed him into the circle, and the two boys danced as Kemp and the crowd clapped in time. Though the boys wore no bells, the audience shouted their praise. Kit felt a pang of regret as he swept off his cap and bowed to the group. Oh, to hear such shouts every day!

When the church bells rang seven, Kemp spoke. "Good men and gentle ladies, the time has come. I, your humble servant Will Kemp, do begin a journey that none has made before. I, who have spent my life in mad jigs and merry jests, do undertake perhaps the maddest" — here he leaped into the air, shaking his bells — "and merriest jig of all. I will dance the morris dance all the way to Norwich." He took a deep bow and the crowd cheered.

"I will miss his mad pranks," said James.

"So will I," said Kit. In his own way, Will Kemp was a great player, nearly equal to Mr. Richard. Perhaps there was not room for two such brilliant stars in a single company. Perhaps a company needed lesser lights and those who were only shadows. Perhaps those shadows and lesser lights allowed stars like Richard Burbage and Will Kemp to shine all the brighter. James wanted to be a star. Kit would try to be content as a shadow.

Will Kemp went on. "I am accompanied by this fine musician, Thomas Slye, who will play for the whole ninety miles." The crowd cheered for Slye, who drummed a measure on the tabor and played upon the pipe.

"Two more faithful servants will also come forth on my journey." One of them took off his cap and passed it around the crowd for a collection.

"That could have been me," whispered James.

Will Kemp continued, "For a shilling you can buy a pair of garters or gloves to commemorate this original event." The second servant handed out the gloves and garters.

Kit marveled at the coins in the cap. London held many prosperous people who would pay a whole shilling for a garter.

When the servant had collected all the money he could get from the crowd, Will Kemp announced, "I, Cavaliero Kemp, headmaster of morris dancers, high head-borough of heigh hos, and only triller of your tra-la-las, and best bell-jangler between Sussex and Scotland, shall begin to frolickly foot it from the hall of the Right Honorable Lord Mayor of London to the Right Worshipful Master Mayor of Norwich." He turned to his musician. "Tickle the tabor, good Tom Slye, and I'll follow thee."

At the sound of the drum and pipe, Will Kemp began to dance. The crowd moved with him as he made his way through the streets. Kit clapped and skipped. Perhaps this mad caper would succeed after all. Perhaps there was a future in dancing. Once again Kit wondered at his place as a stage boy. Was it truly his fate?

The crowd grew so thick Will Kemp could not pass, but his servants opened a path. Kit and James kept up with the merry band as daylight came on and they left the city, passing through Whitechapel and Mile End, finally arriving at the creek at Bow. There Will Kemp stopped to rest. It was time for Kit and James to return to the playhouse.

"'Tis a grand adventure," said Kit as they followed a stream of people heading back toward London.

"'Tis a grand adventure of his own devising," said James. "I do nothing of my own. I get applause, but I need the words of Will Shakespeare, and the art of the other players." He glanced at Kit. "And the stagehands as well."

Kit did not reply. When he returned to the playhouse, he would mix pigments for the artist who was painting a battlefield for Mr.

Shakespeare's new play, *Henry V*. At the end of the day, he would clean the paintbrushes. No glory in that.

"I am the least of the lot," muttered Kit.

James looked at him. "Are you feeling glum?"

Kit trudged along the muddy road and did not answer.

"I confess that I am," declared James. "I want to be with Will Kemp, dancing with bells on, cheered by a crowd. Shall we grumble and groan together?"

Kit laughed, and his gloom vanished. The two boys joked and bantered all the way back to London, adding a hop and skip every now and then.

Runabout

In March gray skies continued to hover over the Curtain playhouse. Along with cleaning the ground and arranging costumes for each day's play, Kit began repairing and painting battered stage properties for Mr. Shakespeare's *Henry V*. Tom gave him his orders, and Kit did his best to please him, or at least to avoid his scowls.

One day Nicholas and James came to the tiring room to try on their costumes.

"Where be the blue princess cloak?" Nicholas asked.

"'Tis on the table, beneath the blue gown," Kit said.

James laughed and said, "You begin to sound like Tom, all growly and such."

Kit frowned.

"Just so, you're miming his scowl as well. Mind how you go, Kit. You need not turn into your master as you learn his skills," said James.

Nicholas gave a sharp laugh. "I knew he was daft from the start."

Kit's scowl deepened. James slapped him on the back and said, "'Tis a friendly quip. Do not take it ill."

After the two boys left, Kit thought of the morning he and James had followed Will Kemp through the city. Though it had been but a few weeks ago, he could feel the gap growing between James and himself.

When the players began to rehearse the new play, the atmosphere grew stormy. As Mr. Shakespeare listened to the players, he changed their lines over and over again.

Mr. Richard, who played King Henry, declared, "I will speak whatever you write, Will. Just make up your mind!"

"I make my mind up anew each time I hear you speak, Richard," Will replied.

Mr. Richard was not amused.

Up on the balcony, Kit smiled as he attached the battlefield painting to ropes so it could be lowered at the proper time. He was not the only one with a dithering mind. Molly saw Kit and waved. He did not wave back. He had not spoken to her since the day of his disgrace.

When he climbed back down to the tiring house, she was sweeping up the pieces of a broken jug and prattling on, though no one else was in the room. "It's all right for some, throwing jugs about, spilling the mead and staining a dress in the bargain. All right if you don't have to make the mead yourself."

She saw Kit, frowned, and kept on. "Heft the water into the pot and onto the fire, boil and stir and stir some more. Skim and strain and then, to please Mr. Richard, go in search of strawberry leaves, violet flowers, and lavender — and just the right balance of ginger and cinnamon, being right careful, for too much ginger makes Mrs. Burbage choke, and then stop it up very close, for if you do not, it will spoil the lot. And then when it is ready, watch careless folks throw it about."

She dropped the broom, and Kit jumped as it clattered to the floor. "Sometimes I do have it up to here" — she tucked her two hands under her chin and stretched her neck as far as she could — "with you players ordering people about as if you were the dukes and lords that you play onstage. Does no one ever think of the grub-slave who does the work so you can go out there and prance about?"

Before Kit could answer, she burst out, "No, none of you do think of her!"

Kit picked up her broom and knocked the handle on the floor. This time it was Molly who jumped. "What am I but a grub-slave?" Kit growled. "I speak no lines; I sing no songs. Grub-slave, thy name is Kit Buckles."

Molly grabbed the broom from his hand. "Oh, but not for long. Soon they will take you on as their 'prentice player. Such a one as you, with your fair hair and red cheeks, you'll be Mr. Shakespeare's new heroine, as soon as you speak your lines to Mister Richard."

Kit turned away from her and walked to the open door that led to the stage. The players had left, and he stared out at the empty playhouse. "I did speak my lines and made a right cobblers of it."

"Oh!" said Molly, silenced for a minute. "What of your dream to be a player?"

"Trampled into the mud out here." He waved his arm toward the ground.

"Did you throw it over after just one try?"

He would not tell Molly of his stage fright, and he would not play the pityhound. "Do you not know? I am a 'prentice stage boy now. The back of the stage is my fate, not the front."

"No, I did not know. Who bothers to tell Molly Godden any news? Perhaps if you tried again —"

Kit kicked the bits of the broken jug and shouted, "My fate is not for you to prate on!"

"Fate, fate — men always talk of their fate." Molly waved her arms about, and her broom clattered to the floor again. "The way the stars move in the heavens, or Lady Fortune turns her wheel and rules our lives. I can't see why the stars should care about you and me.

"The Burbage family has more to say about my fate than the stars. Mr. Richard tells me when to work at the playhouse, and his wife tells me when to tend their children. And if Fortune really is a lady, why does she not treat her own kind better? Why is Fortune's wheel spinning every which way for men, but only one way for girls — to mind a man's house and family while he goes into the wide world to act out his most wondrous fate?"

Kit struggled to make sense of Molly's outrage. "But surely you do believe in fate. 'Tis what makes our lives what they are, and 'tis shown in the stars. You and I can't read them, but wise men can. Mr. Shakespeare does say it so when he calls Romeo and Juliet 'star-crossed lovers.' 'Twas their fate to die."

"No, 'twas not," said Molly. "True, the prologue says so, but see what happens in that play. Will Shakespeare does show us a dozen times when Romeo could choose to ponder his actions, but he does not. Instead Romeo acts rashly, a right fool. If fate makes him do so, then what is the meaning in the story? What is the worth of our lives, if we but speak the lines that fate—or Lady Fortune—has written for us?"

Molly was wondrous clever. If there were no stars, no fate to lead him, did that make things better or worse? Was he truly meant to be a stage boy? Was he wise enough to know?

Molly went on. "I do believe that we are the masters of our fate. Our virtues and faults lie not in the stars, but in ourselves. And I do believe Mr. Shakespeare would agree with me."

They heard a chuckle, and Will Shakespeare stood in the doorway, scribbling on a scrap of paper. "Why, Molly, I do indeed. I see most men — and women too — blundering on their way. If fate and the stars know a better way for them, people do not heed it. As for me —" He snapped his fingers, twirled around, and disappeared from the doorway.

Kit felt his face burn with anger. What did all this clever talk mean? Once again Molly had made him feel a right dolt. He turned to her. "Go and prate on with your wise men about such claptrap. I will hear none of it!"

He returned to the basement and began sanding chipped paint from an old table. He rubbed and scrubbed the rough sandpaper and barely noticed when a sharp splinter pierced his palm. 'Twas not a great fate to be a stage boy, but he was not a great boy. It suited him.

April brought more cold weather. Kit went with Mr. Cuthbert to visit Peter Street.

"'Tis impossible to lay a foundation," said the carpenter. "The ground is still frozen. Even if my men could dig into it, one good frost could heave it up again."

"Mr. Cuthbert moaned. "We are nearly bankrupt! We have sold four of Will Shakespeare's plays to a printer, and that money is gone. Soon we will have to sell our costumes. We *must* be in the playhouse by summer!"

"Tell that to old Jack Frost," said Master Street.

Each time they met, Kit felt sparks fly between the two men.

"You must...."

"I cannot..."

"When...?"

"I do not know...."

"But surely..."

"I can promise nothing."

When the ground finally began to soften, Cuthbert and Richard Burbage saw they had leased a low-lying bog. Will Shakespeare and Peter Street paced the muddy field to decide where to set the playhouse. Kit held the surveying line so Master Street could find the direction of north. Mr. Shakespeare brought calculations from an astronomer that told them where the sun would strike the playhouse at different times of the year.

"I do not want the players squinting," said Mr. Shakespeare. "The stage must always be in shadow."

"Then the audience must squint into the sun," said Peter Street.

"So be it," replied Mr. Shakespeare. "I have played in too many inferior playhouses. This one shall be perfect in every way!"

Peter Street shook his head but said nothing.

Together they talked about the stage doors, the height of the balcony, the width of the trapdoor, the length of the tiring room.

Kit listened to them sparring, like players trading rapier thrusts.

"The new playhouse can be no bigger than the old one," said Peter Street, "for your oak timbers cannot bend like willow branches."

"You must find a way," Mr. Shakespeare said.

Peter Street exclaimed, "Sir, I am a carpenter, not a magician."

When Mr. Shakespeare and Master Street finally reached agreement, they sent Kit to fetch Mr. Richard and Mr. Cuthbert. Then new arguments began.

"I do not like it," said Mr. Richard.

"The cost..." moaned Mr. Cuthbert.

Around and around they went until Kit feared the playhouse would never be built. Meanwhile Peter Street and his men dug trenches to drain the water from the site and sprinkled lime on the ground to mark where the outer and inner walls would be. Whenever Kit could, he stole away from the playhouse to watch the carpenters. They dug the foundation, then set elm pilings in the trench.

"Take a spade and help us," said Peter Street one day.

So Kit helped to fill the trench with limestone and pebbles. "Why do you do this?" he asked.

"The stones will drain water away from the pilings and stop the rot," said Master Street.

Then the bricklayers came to build a foundation wall. But another cold spell stopped work.

"Frost in April?!" thundered Mr. Cuthbert. "'Twill be winter again before we open!" They stood in Peter Street's warehouse, amidst the timbers and beams of the old playhouse.

"Hire all the men you need to do the job," said Mr. Cuthbert. "We are nearly penniless anyway."

"May I borrow this young man as a runabout?" asked Peter Street, looking at Kit. "He proved useful last winter."

Kit broke in. "I would like that, sir."

"Yes, yes!" said Mr. Cuthbert, with a wave of his arm. "Just build the blasted playhouse!"

Back at the Curtain playhouse, Kit told James and Tom of his new work with Master Street.

As he left that day, Molly came up to him. "How fare you, Kit?"

"Well enough," he muttered and pushed past her out the door.

Stripling

In early May Peter Street and his men finally loaded the old beams onto barges and ferried them across the river to Southwark.

"Twenty sides this playhouse will have, just like the old one," said Samuel. "Twenty bays for the inner wall, twenty for the outer. Zounds, what a job!"

Kit marveled at the teams of men with ropes and pulleys, raising the heavy timbers thirty feet into the air. Then carpenters climbed the scaffold with cross frames and curved braces to span the timbers and make each bay secure.

Longer daylight hours meant longer days of work. The sun was up when Kit arrived at the site at six o'clock in the morning. Peter Street was already there, inspecting the work and checking supplies. Kit ran about London with messages to speed the delivery of timber, or hardware, or meat pies for dinner. When the supplies arrived, he checked to see they were correct.

"Have you any building work for me?" Kit asked Samuel one day.

"You would like that, would you? Ask the 'prentices if they need help."

Kit approached a group of young men chiseling pegs from scraps of oak. "Samuel sent me to help," he said.

"Since when did Peter Street take a stripling for a 'prentice?" asked one young man.

"I am not a 'prentice, just a runabout," said Kit. "I can work a chisel though. I am a stage boy 'prentice with the Chamberlain's Men."

"Ha! A spy for the players," said a second young man, slapping his knee. "To see that we don't chisel them!"

They all laughed.

Kit clenched his fists. "I am not a spy," he muttered.

"We need no help from a stripling," said a brawny young man. Kit turned away. First Molly and Nicholas, and now these apprentices. Kit found tormenters in every trade. He felt anger and humiliation, but he dared not show them. Samuel could read his feelings though.

"Did they taunt you?"

Kit muttered, "Prating rogues."

"Carpenters' 'prentices are older than others about town,"

Samuel said. "'Tis the heavy work we do. I was a young one at sixteen. Some are not signed until they are twenty. They do not take kindly to younger boys trying to best them."

"I meant not to best them, but to help," protested Kit.

"I know, but a 'prentice's pride can be right monstrous."

So Kit spent his days fetching tools and supplies for Samuel and the others. He delivered Master Street's angry notes to tardy lumber merchants. He even interrupted Will Shakespeare at his writing. Shakespeare had moved to a room around the corner from the new playhouse.

"Master Street says you must come. He cannot do what you agreed upon," said Kit.

"What think you of our playhouse, Kit?" Mr. Shakespeare asked as they walked to the site.

"'Tis a wondrous marvel. Do you know, sir, that each of the back posts is fitted to twenty-six other timbers from floor to roof? Master Street is a wondrous marvel himself, keeping all the mathematics in his head."

"He is, indeed," said Mr. Shakespeare. "Sometimes I spend an entire day building a frame of words. Next morning I see they are too weak to hold up a scene, let alone a whole play, and I tear them down again. I do envy Master Street. Would that mathematics could help me build a play."

They walked on. Finally Will Shakespeare spoke again. "I mean to call the new playhouse the Globe. I will contain the whole world within that wooden O. What think you of that, Kit?"

"'Twill be a most marvelous world."

"Some poets need brawls and mayhem to fan the flames of their imagination. Ben Jonson murdered a man and went to prison, and brags that his plays are all the better for it. And poor Kit Marlowe was killed in a tavern fight, so wild a life did he crave." A little smile curled his thin lips. "As for me, I need a rather quiet life. To have a palace of a playhouse besides, does well please my muse."

At the end of May, when the frame of the playhouse was nearly complete, the rains came. Rain, rain, and more rain. The river overflowed its banks and flooded the site.

Richard Burbage exclaimed, "Never have I seen such a flood! What did we do to deserve this?" He threw his hands up to heaven and waited for an answer. All he got in reply was a drenched doublet.

"We might as well build a floating playhouse," cried Mr. Shakespeare, "and travel up and down the river."

"'Tis easy to jest," said Mr. Cuthbert, pacing up and down. "Every day costs us more money than we have. Already have I gone to the moneylenders."

Finally, in June, the river fell, the flood drained away, and the sun appeared. The ground dried, and Peter Street began work again. The men set the floor joists and roof rafters. Kit nailed strips of oak lath to form the walls between the timbers. The apprentices took every chance to mock him.

"See the ninny with the hammer!"

Kit struck a blow, missed the nail, and cracked the lath. He felt his face flush with anger.

"Soon he might learn how to use such a tool."

Kit ignored their talk as best he could.

Plasterers came to coat the lath inside and out. Kit counted hundreds of barrels of lime mortar powder, sand, and cow hair that made the rough plaster. Longhaired cows grazed the fields in Suffolk. Would cow hair from his home county find its way to the Globe? Hour after hour the plasterers' apprentices stirred the heavy mix, while others carried pails of it up and down the scaffold where their masters worked.

The building site became a village of masters and apprentices who ran up and down, in and out all day long. The air rang with hammer blows, rasping saws, and shouting men and boys. Samuel planed and Kit sanded rough planks. They laid the stairways, installed the seats, and fitted balusters that held up the railings of the galleries.

The thatchers arrived. Kit helped them count the bundles of Norfolk reeds to cover the roof. The reeds smelled of salty wetlands, a smell from Kit's home by the sea. The Globe contained all parts of Kit's world: Suffolk, London, the players, the builders.

The stage took shape in the center of the huge wooden oval. A dozen men spent a day erecting the four huge columns that would hold up the roof of the stage.

"The columns are hollow, but even so, they must weigh a ton," shouted Samuel.

To Kit it seemed like magic. All these people doing one task at a time, but at the end of each day he could see the changes they had brought. In the center of it all stood Peter Street, master carpenter. Not that he stood still for long. Kit saw him everywhere — on the roof inspecting the thatch, on the scaffold checking the beams, under the stage testing the floor joists, in the gallery adjusting crooked balusters. He still argued with Mr. Richard and Mr. Shakespeare, while Mr. Cuthbert scribbled numbers on a piece of paper.

The June evenings stretched long, and Kit often stayed after the workmen left. In the silence he breathed in the scent of wood shavings and wetland marshes. Master Street stayed late too, and sometimes Kit walked around the playhouse with him as he inspected the work of the day.

"'Tis the biggest building I have ever built," said Peter Street. "It must have been even harder for the master who built the first Theatre. He had no ready-built frame of timbers to guide him. That was twenty-three years ago, when I was but a 'prentice, not much older than you." He climbed onto the stage and knocked on one of the pillars. "I confess I do not sleep well, thinking of all that can go wrong."

"At night I often dream of what I will do the next day," said Kit. "If only..." He trailed off.

"Yes?" asked Peter Street.

"Oh, sir, sometimes I do dream of being a master carpenter like you. I like it much more than being a stage boy, even more than dancing upon the stage."

"It takes more than liking," said Master Street.

"I will work hard. I can do sums, but your geometry I must learn. If only —" Kit paused.

"If only?"

Kit's shoulders slumped. "I gave my word to be a stage boy. I am bound to the Chamberlain's Men."

"You would not be the first boy to change masters."

"Well sir, 'tis not as simple as that. I have come a crooked path." Then Kit told of his journey from the farm fields to the ground on which they stood. He told Master Street of his cutpurse days, his passion for the stage and his frozen fear of speaking lines, his promise to work backstage and his disappointment in the work. "I have made many foolish mistakes," Kit said as he finished his tale.

Peter Street clapped Kit on the back. " 'Tis quite a journey for a boy who is but..." He paused.

"Thirteen last month, sir."

"As for mistakes, we all make them, but not all do confess to them. The Company of Carpenters does not bind apprentices at your age. But we take on boys to do odd jobs and learn the language of the trade. I will give you such a place, if you want it."

Kit's mind whirled. Did he dare to leave the Chamberlain's Men now? He had a certain place there, and a future. James had been tempted to follow Will Kemp, but he had not. If Kit went with Master Street, he could not become a bound apprentice for several years. Perhaps Master Street would not keep him. Perhaps Kit might change his mind again in a year or two and want to be...he knew not what. Was he the sort of boy who would never stick to anything?

Peter Street interrupted Kit's thoughts. "You do not have to answer me now. Think on it. But if you continue to work as you do now, you will be a master carpenter one day. I know enough of the trade and enough of boys to speak truly on that." He held out his hand, and Kit shook it.

Later, Kit stood alone and looked around the unfinished playhouse, from ground to stage to gallery to roof to open sky. He watched the sky turn from deep blue to purple.

"What is it to be?" he shouted, as loud as Mr. Richard would.

"...to be," echoed back to him from the top gallery.

ACT FOURTH, SCENE IV

Friend

As the days went by, questions and thoughts tumbled about inside Kit's head. Would Mr. Cuthbert let him out of his contract? Would Mr. Shakespeare skewer him with wit? Or say nothing but speak disappointment with his piercing eyes? And what if Kit's fancy grew cold? Building the Globe was a wondrous great project. Would he likewise thrill to build a cottage for a shopkeeper?

"Cat got your tongue?" quipped Samuel one day.

Kit started. "I was just thinking. . . ."

"'Tis a bad idea for a boy your size. 'Twill stop you growing taller." He cocked his head. "What do you think about?"

Kit looked at the board he was sanding. His thoughts were too fragile to offer to Samuel. So he replied, "I think how you planed this board to leave as few curls as you may." He picked up a curly wood shaving and twirled it round his finger.

Samuel chattered on. "Myself, I think of the fine dinner I will have tonight at the tavern, and a song afterward." He began to sing;

"Why doth not my goose
sing as well as thy goose
when I paid for my goose
twice as much as thine?"

Kit sang along with Samuel. Perhaps his answer would come with less thinking.

One day at the Curtain playhouse door, someone grabbed him from behind and threw something over his head. Kit struggled to free himself. Was it Roger come to kidnap him? When he could see again, he saw that 'twas a dress pulled over his shirt. James thrust a pair of lady's slippers into his hand. "Quickly, you must join the dance at the end of this act," he said.

As Kit skipped the familiar steps across the stage, he felt the old thrill of a player's life. Perhaps he could be a hired player — as long as he had no lines to speak. Later, back at the building site, as he sanded the oak banisters, he felt an inner glow that matched the golden wood touched by the evening sun.

Why could he not discover his fate? He looked up at the sky, framed by the huge wooden O of the Globe. A wispy cloud drifted by, but no thunderbolt, no voice from the heavens. He sometimes felt as muddy as Mr. Shakespeare's character Bottom, who didn't even notice when his own head was switched for a donkey's head. He felt his face and laughed. Good! He still had his own head, however muddy it might be.

July arrived with the glaziers, who put in windows. The carpenters had a hundred small jobs to complete. But in a few weeks the Chamberlain's Men would move in. One day Samuel sent Kit to Peter Street's warehouse. "Peg together the frames that I finished yesterday. I must know if they all fit before we bring them to the site. They are meant for a cottage behind the playhouse."

At the warehouse, Kit sorted through the lumber Samuel had cut. Each beam had a special notch that matched its mate. One end of a beam had a rectangular hole — a mortise — cut in it; the end of another beam had a narrow part — a tenon — that fit into the hole. Kit found the matching beams and joined them together. Some of these mortise and tenon joints needed the blow of a hammer to make them fit; others slid in smoothly.

When Kit finished joining the frame, he ran his hand over the sweet-smelling wood, not long since brought from the forest. A carpenter must understand the tree and see the finished beams within the trunk. He must know how to make those beams carry the load of floors, roof, and walls. Kit had so much to learn before he became a master carpenter, and even now Master Street came across puzzles to solve in his work.

It would take a lifetime to learn the carpenters' trade. And suddenly Kit knew. That life would fit him like the mortise and tenon joints laid out before him. 'Twas his fate to be a carpenter. All his doubts vanished like the steam from a boiling kettle.

Bang! Bang!

He began to hammer pegs into holes in the fitted beams. With each blow his mind grew clearer. His weeks working at the Globe had been the happiest since he came to London.

Bang! Bang!

"What are you doing here?"

Kit whirled around to see Molly standing in the doorway, hands on her hips.

"What are *you* doing here?" he snapped back, his calmness vanished.

"Why do you not work anymore?"

Kit spoke between clenched teeth. "I do work, as you can plainly see."

"But . . . you ran away from us again." She walked toward him.

Kit did not reply as he took up a scrap of oak to chisel a new peg. He jabbed at the wood and the peg split in two. Throwing it as hard as he could, he nearly hit a raven perched in the rafters. The bird squawked, flapped its wings, and flew off.

Kit grabbed his hammer and another peg. "Go away, Molly."

Bang! Kit drove the peg into the beam.

"Leave."

Bang!

"Me."

Bang!

"Alone."

Molly marched over to Kit and grabbed him by the shoulders. He looked down at her crooked hand.

"Kit, look at me."

He looked at his hammer instead.

"Look at me!"

He raised his eyes to hers.

"Why are you angry with me? What have I done?"

Kit said nothing and looked away. He would not speak of all the times she had made him feel a right fool, for then he would feel so again.

"What is wrong with you?" she asked.

"Nothing."

"You speak not truly."

"I work for Master Street to help build the Globe playhouse," he said fiercely, "and I will become his 'prentice when I am older."

Molly glowered. "Is that why you ran away?" she asked.

Kit continued, "I did not run away. Mr. Cuthbert knows where I am. So does Mr. Shakespeare."

"Why did you leave without telling the rest of us?"

"Who would care? Nicholas was doubtless glad to see me go, and Tom only scowls at me. Anyway, Tom does know."

Bang! He beat a peg into a hole. "I tried to do the work of a stage boy. I tried to be like you, Molly, happy with my lot —"

Bang!

"— but I failed. I cannot be a player. I will not be a stage boy. I want to build real things, not stage properties. My grandsire built ships, and I help to build a playhouse as grand as any ship. That is my fate, I know it." He moved to the next beam. He could feel Molly looking at him.

Bang! Bang!

Finally, in between blows of the hammer, Molly spoke barely above a whisper. "You said no one would care that you left. 'Tis not true."

Kit looked up to catch her words.

She rubbed her crooked hand. "I wanted to be your friend from the first." She giggled. "Well, not when I sat on you."

Kit frowned. Would she never stop teasing?

Molly continued. "Do not frown. 'Tis your pityhound barking again. When we met at the apple market, you said it truly. I did want to help you most, not the players. When you learned the part of Beatrice, did not I help you?"

"You had little good to say, but laughed at what I did." Kit picked up a handful of wooden pegs and pretended to study them.

She went on, her voice soft again. "I did not laugh at you, but at the pleasure of helping you. I do not laugh to shame you or anyone. Though few pay me any mind at the playhouse."

Kit looked up in surprise. "You always seem so cheerful."

"A girl can be cheerful and still want a friend."

They stood in silence. Had he got Molly all wrong?

Finally he spoke. "Master Street told me that the Queen used all the best timber in England for the ships that my grandsire built to defeat the Spanish Armada, when you and I were but infants. What trees be left now are not so tall and cost dearly. That is why we had to save the timbers from the old playhouse to build the new one."

Molly looked at Kit with a puzzled expression.

"Do you not see? There is a link between the Spanish king back then and myself today. Between my grandsire's fate and my own — and all of you at the players' company, and we who build the new playhouse."

Kit smiled at Molly. Perhaps he was not a witless ninnyhammer after all. "I do not know how many strands twist together to make the thread that is our life — the Spanish invasion and my grandsire, and your father who left you, and how we both found our way to this warehouse on this day. Who is spinning all those threads?"

"A giant spider!" exclaimed Molly.

Kit smiled.

"If Giles Allen had not locked us out, you would not have met Peter Street," said Molly.

"If you had not tripped me and sat on me..." added Kit.

They looked at each other and laughed.

"Only a poet like Mr. Shakespeare can untangle such a web," said Molly, "though I still would not call it fate."

"You are a stubborn girl," said Kit.

"Nearly a match for you?" She smiled and stood up. "Whether 'tis fate or my own choosing, I shall go home now and give the Burbage children their supper — if I do not get kicked by a horse on the way. And if you ever finish building the playhouse, I will be there with my apples on the opening day, and sell them to all who give me a farthing. Yet much else might happen instead...."

"If fate be kind, on opening day I will buy an apple from you," said Kit.

Changeling

After Kit finished his work at the warehouse, he went to see Mr. Cuthbert. He had gone often, delivering messages from Peter Street. Today he would deliver a message of his own.

"Well, Kit, what do you have for me today?" asked Mr. Cuthbert. "A vexing problem or a good report?"

"Neither, sir." Kit let his eyes flit all around the familiar room, anywhere but on the face of Mr. Cuthbert. "Well, sir, perhaps it may be both. I think it a good report, but perhaps I mistake it, and 'tis or will be a problem. Or perhaps 'tis a problem for one of us and a good report for the other."

"Come, come, speak plainly." Mr. Cuthbert leaned on his elbows.

Kit took a deep breath. "Sir, I wish to leave the playhouse and go to Master Street. I cannot be a 'prentice yet, but Master Street promises me a place as a runabout until I am old enough to sign the papers."

Mr. Cuthbert opened his eyes wide. "I seem to recall you signed a contract to learn the trade of a stage-keeper. Your mind was set on it."

Kit met his gaze. "'Twas, sir, until I was sent to the new playhouse. The work suits me very well, and Master Street says I have a knack for it. . . . I do like it more than —" He stopped, not wanting to offend.

Mr. Cuthbert nodded for a long time. Finally he spoke. "Peter Street is a good man, though his temper does rise to boiling at times." He chuckled. "But then whose temper does not?"

Kit waited for a moment and then said, "You have been most kind to me, sir."

Mr. Cuthbert blinked. "You are a credit to yourself, young man. I shall be sorry to see you go, but I wish you well with Master Street. I will draw up your release, and you and I will sign it."

Mr. Cuthbert stood up and held out his hand. Kit shook it hard. "I thank you, sir, for all you —" He felt his throat swell and dared not speak more. He turned and hurried out the door.

Made bold by his meeting with Mr. Cuthbert, Kit ran across London Bridge, all the way to Mr. Shakespeare's door. He knocked three times.

"Come in."

Kit opened the door. Mr. Shakespeare, as always, was bent over a table, writing.

"Not another problem! What is wrong now — the hinges on the trapdoor or the steepness of the stairs to the attic?" Mr. Shakespeare kept writing.

"Nothing at the playhouse." Kit swallowed. "Nothing at all, really. I come only to tell you something of myself."

Finally Mr. Shakespeare put down his pen and turned to face Kit.

Kit blurted out, "I have made up my mind to become a carpenter and work for Master Peter Street as a runabout until such time as he will bind me as an apprentice, in five or six years. Before then I mean to learn geometry and all else that Master Street will teach me."

Mr. Shakespeare wove his fingers together, put them behind his head, and leaned back in his chair. "Well, Kit, how came this to be?"

Kit saw that he was not angry, and so he smiled. "Since I began to work for Master Street at the Globe, nay, even last winter when we took apart the Theatre, I have warmed to the carpenter's trade. I do like the sound of the plane smoothing a plank, giving off a whiff of the oak tree. I do like the hundred details to be thought of each day. 'Tis work that will satisfy my heart and my head.

"Why come tell me, the hired scribbler?" Mr. Shakespeare smiled and crossed his arms on his chest.

Kit looked into his eyes. "You told me once that I had spirit. You have been kind to me, since that day last autumn.... You told me to dance, and I did, but not to Norwich with Will Kemp."

Mr. Shakespeare laughed.

"I have discovered that the stage of my world is to be the carpenters' hall. I did not know my own mind until now. Or is it my fate I now know?" Kit moved two steps closer to the desk that was awash in paper.

Mr. Shakespeare wrinkled his brow and searched amongst his papers until he came upon a scrap and read, "'We are the masters of our fate. Our virtues and faults lie not in the stars, but in ourselves.' Now where did I hear that?"

"'Twas Molly."

"Ah yes. That girl has her wits about her."

Kit did not want to talk about Molly's wits. "Sir, I hope you will not think me 'a fickle changeling and a poor discontent.'"

Will Shakespeare clapped his hands. "You listen well to my lines. No, Kit, you are a fair promising changeling."

Kit saw a sheet of paper on the floor with inkblots and crossed-out lines. "That paper tells me you do change your mind too, sir. I have heard you change it even as Mr. Richard speaks your lines."

Mr. Shakespeare laughed. "So I do, so I do. And so do we all." Then he grew serious. "I have watched you, Kit, even as you have watched me. I am glad to see you find your way with coolness of mind and warmth of heart. That way lies mastery of any trade — and any fate."

He stood up and put both hands on Kit's shoulders. "I hope to see you a master carpenter and a citizen of London when you are grown. Or will you take your skills and return to Suffolk?"

"I do not know, sir. I cannot see that far."

"Good lad! Do not stumble by looking too far down the road. Yet mind you watch the scenes as you pass."

"Do you write a play for the new playhouse, sir?"

"I do. 'Tis about Julius Caesar, who lived and died long ago, but whose story I write for our modern times."

"I shall come and see it at the Globe," said Kit. "I have got a fancy for plays and will see them all, if Master Street will let me."

"You give me an idea, Kit." He sat down at his table, dipped his quill in the ink, and scribbled some words. Without looking up, he said, "Look for a line I write for you and your fellow carpenters."

"Me, sir? You write about me?"

"Just a line. Look you for it."

"I thank you, sir," said Kit as he left Will Shakespeare to his words.

ACT FIFTH

Dancer

"A penny for the ground! See the wondrous new playhouse! I thank you, madam." Tom, doing duty as a gatherer, stood mobbed by people eager to see the first play at the Globe. Kit and Master Street, along with his carpenters and apprentices, pushed their way to the entrance.

"Which play will we see?" asked an apprentice.

"*Julius Caesar*, a new one by Mr. Shakespeare," replied Kit.

Peter Street gave Tom half a crown. "Ten seats in the upper gallery."

Tom looked at Master Street and his party. His eyes settled on Kit. "Going to pay today, are you?"

Kit clenched his fists. Would people never forget his crime? Then he saw Tom's smile, a thin smile to be sure, but a smile. Kit smiled back. He was learning to cool his temper, but it would take him time to learn the lesson well.

"Only the best seats for my men," said Master Street. "We want a good look at our work."

Kit followed Master Street up to the top gallery, rubbing his hands along the smooth railing as he went. He saw Molly down below, with a basket of apples. "Molly!" he shouted.

She looked about her on the ground.

"Molly, up here!" Kit shouted again, but she did not look up.

"Here is threepence for some apples," said Peter Street.

Kit clambered down the stairs again, squeezing through the tide of people surging upward. When he finally reached the ground, Molly was nowhere in sight, so he went looking for her.

Then he stopped short. Roger stood whispering to Ginger and Big Ears, the two boys who had attacked Kit last winter. Kit ducked behind a stout man to hide. After a minute or two, Roger sauntered away from the boys, who stayed close together and looked nervously at the growing crowd.

Kit thought of that day last autumn when he had come to cut purses. He remembered the fearful flutter in his belly. What if he had not got caught? He might be standing here today, ready to cut more purses. He looked down at his leather apron. He and the carpenters had come in their working clothes. Kit was proud of his apron. He glanced around the Globe playhouse, still smelling faintly of new lumber, the plaster fresh and clean. He looked up to see the thatched roof shining golden in the sunlight, framing an oval of bright blue sky.

Brrm, ba ba brrm! A trumpet sounded, announcing the play. Kit looked at Ginger and Big Ears. What roads would they travel?

"Apples, get them 'fore they are gone!" Molly's voice called above the din.

Kit hurried over to her.

"Well, Master Christopher Buckles. Come to see your pride and joy?" She swept her arm wide around the playhouse.

"That I am, Mistress Molly Godden. I would like threepence worth of apples for our men, sitting in the top gallery."

She raised her eyebrows. "Are we not grand!"

Kit grinned. "'Tis Master Street celebrating, just for today. Next time I come — if I have a free afternoon and a penny — I'll be a groundling."

Brrm, ba ba brrm! The trumpet sounded again. Kit gave Molly the money and folded the apples into his apron. He leaned close to her. "See those two boys over there, standing together?" They had not moved since Roger left them.

Molly nodded. "Who are they?"

"Part of Roger's gang. I think they mean to cut purses, so keep your eye on them."

"I'll stick to them like glue. But we do need an apprentice stage boy," she said. Kit gave a laugh, then hurried back up the stairs.

"I thought you had got lost," said Peter Street.

"I saw some lads I know," said Kit.

A few players walked out onstage.

"*Hence! home, you idle creatures get you home,*" said the first man, dressed in a Roman toga.

"*Is this a holiday? What! know you not,*

Being mechanical, you ought not walk

Upon a laboring day without the sign

Of your profession? Speak, what trade art thou?"

"*Why, sir, a carpenter,*" said a second man.

The first man stared at him. "*Where is thy leather apron and thy rule?*

What dost thou with thy best apparel on?"

Kit grinned. Mr. Shakespeare had done it — given him a line, a line that players would say each time the play was presented. And *Julius Caesar* might last as long as this great Globe playhouse would last, maybe even longer.

The carpenters left the stage, and Kit was swept back to ancient Rome and a bloody tale of betrayal, murder, and revenge. He smiled when one player repeated Molly's lines near exactly. "*Men at some time are masters of their fates. The fault, dear Brutus, is not in our stars, but in ourselves. . . .*" He gasped when Caesar was killed by his friends. He nearly cried when James, playing Portia, begged her husband not to fall on his sword. And he thrilled when Mark Antony turned the mob his way.

When the play was over, the crowd clapped and cheered for the players. Kit also heard cries for Will Kemp.

"Where is the jig then?"

"We want Will Kemp!"

But Mr. Richard and the others ignored them and took many bows. Nicholas and James, playing Roman wives, received cheers and whistles too.

Peter Street sent the rest of the crew back to work, but took Kit to the tiring house to greet the players. James had removed his long gown to look at the hem. "I tripped going onstage and tore it," he said to Kit. "I trust you do not do much sewing now. Those arms wield something heavier than a needle."

Kit glanced at his arms.

"Ah, the girls will like those muscles," teased James.

Kit blushed and looked around. "Where is Molly?"

"Here I am," she said, coming up behind him. "I stuck so close to your two boys they left during Act Two with nothing to show for it."

Kit smiled. "I thank you, Molly. Did you hear your lines that Mr. Shakespeare borrowed? Perhaps 'tis your fate to be a poet!"

Molly blushed, then sighed.

"Why not?" asked Kit. "You are clever enough. Our own Queen writes poems, 'tis said. You can be mistress of your fate."

Molly blushed more and slipped away.

Kit saw Will Shakespeare talking to Peter Street. They both turned and looked toward him. Then Mr. Shakespeare shook hands with Master Street and walked over to Kit. "What think you of my new play?"

"'Twas most marvelous, sir. You made each man both true and false. I could not tell who to love and who to hate."

"Then I did what I set out to do," Mr. Shakespeare said. "You have a sharp ear as well as shoulders grown broad." He put a hand on Kit's shoulder. "I have written another play about the confusions of love, and I am toiling with another about a young man who knows not which way to turn. I feel a new fire burning in me."

"Not so hot as to strike the thatch, I hope," said Kit.

Will Shakespeare threw back his head and laughed. "The winds that fan my fire come from many directions. Richard Burbage and the others are the best players in the world. A playwright could ask for no better. But your playhouse kindles my imagination too, Kit."

Kit looked at his shoes. He had not yet learned to feel easy with praise. "'Tis not my playhouse, sir."

"Ah, but your mark is on it. You beat the pegs and sanded the planks. You have a right to feel proud." He took a drink of wine from a goblet. "How do you fare with Peter Street?"

Kit said, "I fare well, sir. You build palaces with words. I will build cottages out of wood. But I feel some sparks of a fire, if I may say so."

"Of course you may." Will Shakespeare put his arm around Kit's shoulder. "You have spirit. I saw it from the first, and it has served you well. A stroll through an open field on a summer's day — where is the challenge in that? We have climbed some rocky hills and entered dark caves, you and I, and there be more to come, I trow. But they will not keep us from dancing."

This talk of fires and dark caves make Kit's head spin. Yet it made a goodly kind of sense too.

Will Shakespeare went on. "We each have our own road to travel. But once in a while they may meet and when they do, let us dance together."

"'Twould please me right well, sir," said Kit.

A player had struck up a tune on the tabor and pipe on the stage. Will Shakespeare took Kit's hand, whirled him around once, and then left him.

Kit skipped to the center of the stage where Nicholas and James, a few of the players, and Molly had gathered in a circle. Kit slipped in beside her, caught the beat of the tabor, and began to dance in time with the others.

✤ AUTHOR'S NOTE ✤

My inspiration for *All the World's a Stage: A Novel in Five Acts* came from history: the deconstruction of the Theatre playhouse in December 1598, and its rebuilding as the Globe in 1599. The dramatic events and colorful cast of characters led me to imagine the story through the eyes of a boy.

Though Kit Buckles is my own creation, most of the characters in the book really lived and played roles in this grand adventure — William Shakespeare, Richard and Cuthbert Burbage, Will Kemp, Augustine Phillips, Peter Street, Giles Allen, and Henry Johnson, as well as two boy players, Nicholas Tooley and James Sands. Their personalities and the lines they speak are my invention, except Will Kemp's speeches in Act IV, Scene I, which he wrote in a book about his marathon morris dance.

Kit's family name, Buckles, is most commonly found in his home county of Suffolk. Molly's name, Godden, was my English grandfather's family name. He immigrated to America in 1906, and I'd like to think we had an ancestor as brave and clever as Molly.

I remained true to the weather conditions of the time: the snowstorm on the first day of the demolition in December 1598, the frost in April 1599, the floods in May, and the sunshine in June. Will Kemp did dance all the way to Norwich, though a year later than I place it. The Globe did open with Shakespeare's new play *Julius Caesar* in late summer, *1599*. As for its first lines, no one knows what — or who — inspired them.

Some of my research came from dozens of books about Elizabethan London, Shakespeare and his company, and the lives of apprentices. More research was done by bicycle on the streets of London, locating landmarks of Kit's adventures. An interview with the historian at the Worshipful Company of Carpenters (which has occupied the same plot of land since *1429*) and a private backstage tour of Shakespeare's Globe Theatre gave me close-up details for the book. But most wondrous of all were Shakespeare's plays that I saw at the Globe, which still resound with the passion and promise that was Elizabethan England.

Coat of Arms of
the Worshipful Company
of Carpenters

✷ GLOSSARY ✺

ballad — poem printed on one sheet of paper, called a broadside, reporting news of crimes and scandals

baluster — upright support for a railing

beef-brained — thickheaded, stupid

bill — weapon with curved blade and long wooden handle

blessed pudding! — good gracious!

bookkeeper — person who stood backstage and prompted players who forgot their lines

brass — boldness, nerve

bullyrag — to insult or intimidate

bung — purse that men wore tied to their waists

cobblers — botched job, failure

cove — young fellow

cutpurse — thief who stole purses

doublet — jacket worn by men

drudge — someone who did unpleasant, dull, or hard work

farthing — coin worth one-fourth of a penny

fishmonger — seller of fish

gatherer — man or woman who collected money at a playhouse

grandame — grandmother

grandsire — grandfather

groundlings — playgoers who stood on the ground, on three sides of
the stage

grub-slave — lowly worker

guild — organization of tradesmen that made rules for their profession

halberd — weapon with axe blade and long spike

How now? — What's this? What's going on?

Jack-sauce — impudent fellow

jig — skit, songs, and dances, often rude or bawdy, performed at the end of a play

joist — one of a set of parallel beams that held up a floor or ceiling

jolthead — stupid person

lath — web of sticks or nailed boards between beams that formed a backing for plaster

Master of the Revels — government official who censored all plays

muse — originally a Greek goddess who inspired learning and the arts; anything that inspires a poet or an artist

my eyes — exclamation of surprise

ninnyhammer — fool, blockhead

nip — steal

nought — nothing

perchance — maybe

pipe — flute

playbook — the script of a play, divided into many "books," each
    containing a scene

prate — to speak foolishly, boastfully, or chatter on and on

premium — a fee paid for an apprenticeship

properties — scenery and other "props" for plays

rapier — long sword with a double-edged blade

rogue — idle vagrant, scoundrel

shipwright — shipbuilder

stage-keeper — one who works backstage, building props and
    arranging special effects

stow you — shut up

strike a peg — beat up

stripling — an adolescent boy

Theatre — playhouse built by the Burbage family in 1576 and torn down in 1598

thribble — improvised dialogue, not written into the script

tiring house — backstage room where costumes and props were stored

trow — believe, suppose

wench — young woman (sometimes used as an insult)

wherryman — boatman on a wherry, or light rowing boat, used for passengers and goods

Worshipful Company of Carpenters — carpenters' guild formed in 1271

zounds — wow

SELECTED BIBLIOGRAPHY

Books

Chrisp, Peter, *Eyewitness: Shakespeare*. New York: DK Children, 2004. Full of illustrations of life and theatre in Shakespeare's time.

Kemp, William, *Kemps Nine Daies Wonder: Performed in a daunce from London to Norwich*. London: Camden Society, 1840. You can download a copy on http://books.google.com.

Langley, Andrew, *Shakespeare's Theatre*. New York: Oxford University Press, 1999. Also available in paperback (Oxford, 2000). Illustrated story of the first Globe Theatre and its recent reconstruction in London.

Morley, Jacqueline, *Shakespeare's Theater*. New York: Peter Bedrick Books, 1994. Also available in paperback (Hodder Wayland, 1998). Illustrated history of the Lord Chamberlain's Men.

Picard, Liza, *Elizabeth's London: Everyday Life in Elizabethan London*. New York: St. Martin's Press, 2003. Also available in paperback (St. Martin's, 2005). Details of life in all social classes.

Shapiro, James, *A Year in the Life of William Shakespeare: 1599*. New York: HarperCollins, 2005. A scholarly book about what Shakespeare did in 1599 and what was happening around him.

WEB SITES

These Web sites were active at the date of publication.

http://www.absoluteshakespeare.com. This Web site is especially comprehensive.

http://shakespeare.palomar.edu. This Web site is also known as *Mr. William Shakespeare and the Internet*.

http://www.renfaire.com. Listings of Renaissance Faires all over North America are included, with sections on food, costume, language, games, history, etc. There's enough information here to stage your own Renaissance Faire.

FILMS/DVDS

Many filmed versions of Shakespeare's plays are available at public libraries. The following series includes all thirty-seven of his plays: BBC *Shakespeare Plays*, London: BBC / Time Life, 2000.